Mills & Boon Best Seller Romance

A chance to read and collect some of the best-loved novels from Mills & Boon – the world's largest publisher of romantic fiction.

Every month, four titles by favourite Mills & Boon authors will be re-published in the *Best Seller Romance* series.

A list of other titles in the *Best Seller Romance* series can be found at the end of this book.

Mary Wibberley

BELOVED ENEMY

MILLS & BOON LIMITED
LONDON · TORONTO

First published 1973

ISBN 0 263 73492 7

Set in 11/12 pt Linotype Baskerville

Made and printed in Great Britain by
Richard Clay (The Chaucer Press) Ltd, Bungay, Suffolk

CHAPTER ONE

'My dear,' said Great-Aunt Margaret, 'I'm so pleased you've come at last. And you must stay as long as you like.' Her hand patted Holly's, and Holly smiled and looked at her with affection.

'I've always loved it here. I feel as if I'm coming home – and now, since Mother died —' her voice faltered, and she blinked furiously, looking ahead through the windscreen of the Mini at the fine Highland rain that had begun as she had left the train at Strathmhor station.

'I know, child. It's not been easy. But the house is sold now. You've no ties. Your mother, rest her soul, wouldn't want you to grieve any more. You must make your home with me here for as long as it suits you. Thank heaven I phoned when I did.'

Holly, sitting beside her, thought back to the phone call the previous afternoon. She so nearly hadn't answered it, sunk as she was in despondency. And when she'd heard Aunt Margaret's voice, she had poured out her troubles in a sudden rush because of the kindness and sympathy in her aunt's tone, told her about being dismissed from her job the day before because she had repulsed the boss's son once too often – and a shade too firmly for his or his father's liking – and had walked out, even as his maddened voice had followed her: 'Don't bother to come back, Miss Templeton.'

'Don't worry,' she'd managed to retort. 'You didn't tell me I'd need to have a black belt in judo to work here! You can send my cards by post.' And she'd slammed the door, leaving Mr. Andrews and Sandy to pick up the broken vase and mop the water from her once tidy desk. The brief satisfaction at her gesture of defiance had been short-lived. And when she had reached home she had wept, feeling truly alone again. Her mother had died five months previously, and the house was sold, nearly all the furniture too, and on Monday she would move into a flat with two friends, Jane and Sarah. Only now she wouldn't be moving in at all . . . she was travelling instead to her aunt's home in the remote Highlands.

'How could anyone be so *stupid*!' her aunt exclaimed as she swept past a lorry with inches to spare, spattering their windscreen profusely with muddy rain. Holly closed her eyes. It made the journey less hazardous somehow. Aunt Margaret's driving was only slightly less eccentric than her appearance, and if you couldn't actually see the telegraph posts or lorries leaping out at you, then travelling with her could be accomplished with less wear and tear on the nerves. Not quite sure whether her aunt referred to the lorry driver who had not unnaturally blasted his horn, or her boss's behaviour, Holly asked: 'How are the animals?'

Aunt Margaret took her eyes from the narrow road, now almost invisible through the fine brown film obscuring her windscreen.

'What? The animals? Oh, fine. Just splendid. Of course, we've had a couple of additions since last I saw you. Er—' she stopped abruptly and looked at Holly with a sweet smile, swerving slightly as a result.

'Oh? How many?' Holly braced her legs, and felt the seat belt just to make sure it was secure.

'Well, some kittens arrived. I couldn't do anything but keep them, they're so *sweet*.'

'Arrived? You mean one of the cats gave birth?'

'Oh, no!' she laughed. 'I found them in a cardboard box – or rather, Gareth did.' She was suddcnly busy changing gears as they neared a tricky bend in the road, and Holly waited, a question hovering on her lips.

Aunt Margaret collected animals and lame dogs, four or two-footed, the way some people collect stamps. And in the same way that abandoned babies are found on orphanage steps, so were abandoned animals found in her porch. She was known for miles around as the 'Animal Lady', the word 'mad' being added by the less charitable, and fortunately very rare, ones. But Gareth? Holly frowned. Surely not a dog – or a horse?

Safely on a stretch of fairly straight road, she ventured to ask: 'Who is Gareth?'

'Ah, yes. Well, you know my other cottage?'

Holly's heart sank. 'Yes?'

'Well, he's – er – staying there for a while.'

'A man?'

Aunt Margaret managed to look both vague and puzzled at the same time, no mean feat, even for her. 'Well, yes! But he's a big help. He does odd jobs and things, and feeds the animals if I have to go out – you know.' She took her left arm away from the wheel to gesture carelessly. It didn't deceive Holly for a moment.

'Oh, Aunt Margaret! Not another one. How did you find him?'

'Well, he just arrived one day in a battered-looking Land-Rover and asked if I knew who owned the empty cottage near mine. I told him I did, and he asked if it was for sale. To cut a long story short – I'm sure you don't want me to go into detail, you look so *tired* after that long journey from Manchester, dear – he's renting it off me for a few months.' And she turned on the car radio in a way that meant, I do not wish to talk about it any more.

Holly bit her lip. Perhaps, she thought, it was a good thing that she was going to stay there for a while. She'd met some of the lame dogs that her aunt couldn't resist helping, and most of them had seemed instinctively to be the type to take advantage of a dear, kind-hearted old lady. One, a couple of years previously, had helped himself to some irreplaceable family heirlooms before vanishing early one morning, and Aunt Margaret had refused to tell the police. 'No,' she had said. 'Perhaps the poor man needed help – and what use were the ornaments anyway? I never did like that statue, ugly thing that it was.'

She lived alone in a rambling white cottage with outbuildings, quite a mile from the nearest road, with only the animals for company. If some strange man was living in the other cottage, Holly decided she wanted to see him.

'Nearly there.' Aunt Margaret tooted vigorously as they went up the narrow twisting street of Kishard, by the loch that gleamed leadenly in the misty rain, and villagers turned and waved, their faces creasing into smiles when they recognized the car. Nearly everyone there loved her, and if they had any sense, kept well out of the way when she came flying into the village twice a week on her bike for the groceries. The brown tweed tartan-lined cloak that she wore winter and summer gave her a dramatic appearance, and Holly had once heard her pointed out by a local to a gaping American tourist as: 'Miss Templeton herself, our local celebrity,' said in soft admiring Highland tones. The villagers never forgot that she had written poems and children's stories in her younger, teaching days.

They swept out of the village, along the tree-lined road to the cottage, turned off a mile later and bumped up the steep winding track that led its hilly way to Rhu-na-Bidh, 'House of the Elms', her home. Higher and higher they went, and somehow, as always for Holly, it was like returning home again. Very quietly she said: 'Thank you, Aunt Margaret.'

Her aunt nodded. 'That's all right, child. You know I love to have you here.' And then they were there. Aunt Margaret swerved to avoid the great Alsatian that leapt from the barn, barking furiously and wagging his tail. He looked vicious, but was as soft as butter. She had rescued him, a starving shivering puppy, from a gang of louts three years previously on one of her rare ventures to Edinburgh, and for him there was no one else in the world. He even tolerated all the other animals because he sensed they were precious to her.

'Down, Kazan, don't cover Holly with your muddy paws,' Aunt Margaret said firmly as they got out of the orange Mini, and he rolled over on the wet path, overcome with delight. Holly went to the boot to collect her cases, unable to resist a look at the white cottage nestling in the elms a few dozen yards away. Smoke curled from the chimney, and someone had put red curtains at the windows. Holly bit her lip as she looked at her aunt going towards the door. She would never change. If it wasn't 'Gareth', no doubt it would be someone else. There was always someone wanting help, in need of a meal or a bed, and she had a big heart, unable to resist a plea for help. Holly closed her eyes for a second. 'Who am I to talk?' she wondered. 'Am I not just such a one?' She picked up her luggage and followed her aunt into the house.

The living room was warm and welcoming, the fire newly stoked up. Aunt Margaret looked approvingly round at Holly. 'There now, he's been in and built up the fire for us. Wasn't that thoughtful?'

'You mean—' Holly put down her cases on the thick red carpet, '—he just comes in and out as he wants?'

'Why, yes. He knew I was going to meet you—'

'But you don't *know* him! He could—' she gestured helplessly round, unable to finish.

'He's got an honest face. I know people. Now, the kettle. Sit down, I'll make you a nice cup of tea.'

Holly followed her aunt into the kitchen, remembering just in time to duck her head in the low doorway. She was too agitated to sit down. 'But you could come home to find everything gone!' She put her hand to her head. Perhaps she hadn't arrived a moment too soon. 'Where does he come from, this Gareth?'

'Heavens, I don't know! What does it matter? He pays his rent regularly, does lots of odd jobs – and he's clean and sober,' and she paused, and gave her niece an oddly speculative glance. Holly was to discover what that look meant, but not until a long time after.

'I'm sorry, Aunty,' she said. 'I don't know what's the matter with me. It's just that I don't like to see you hurt or anything.'

'I know. You've been under a strain these last few months as well. Have a look at the kittens. Aren't they beauties?'

Holly bent to the large cardboard box in which slept

five fluffy ginger kittens, hardly more than four weeks old. One woke, and stretched, looking at her curiously. She bent and picked it up, feeling the sharp little claws digging into her sweater as it began to purr.

'Oh, it's lovely! How could anyone leave them like that?' she exclaimed.

'I don't know, but they did. At least they brought them here instead of drowning them, poor wee things. Give them some milk, child, then put them out in the run at the back for a while.'

As Holly busied herself lifting them out, a soft warm nose was pressed into her neck, and she turned to greet Smokey, the big black labrador. She was old now, nearly twelve, and a little rheumaticky, and of all her aunt's animals she was Holly's favourite. She greeted her, then the two tabbies, Bunty and Kitty, who also lived in the house, and who, hearing the arrival, had come down to investigate.

On her previous visits, Holly had grown used to waking in the middle of the night to find one or more animals soundly asleep on her bed, usually in such a position that she could barely move.

'We'll feed them all in a little while, but first, a drink of tea,' and she passed Holly a steaming cup. She shooed the kittens and cats outside and shut the door.

'I don't know how you manage,' Holly told her aunt as they settled down by the fire for a few precious minutes.

'Och, they're no trouble once you get used to them. Gareth has been building pens in the stable for the others, the strays. It'll be a relief knowing they're warm in winter, and there really are too many for the house.'

Holly repressed a smile. Aunt Margaret would have given up her bed rather than think any animal was cold. This Gareth seemed to know what he was about, she reflected wryly. Anyone who shared her aunt's love of animals was beyond reproach – or was he just shrewd enough to guess that? She would soon know. Aunt Margaret was old, and always saw the best in everyone. Holly, at eighteen, didn't share her trusting faith. She was already forming a mental picture of the stranger, the intruder, and it was a disquieting one.

There was still no sign of him after they had eaten their evening meal. At nine o'clock, Aunt Margaret always took the dogs for a walk, and as the two of them walked to the barn clad in wellingtons and macs, Holly ventured to ask: 'Doesn't – er – Gareth come to see you at all?'

Her aunt gave a throaty chuckle. 'Want to meet him, eh? I dare say he's keeping out of the way for today, knowing I've got a visitor.'

'You told him I was coming?' Holly asked.

'Yes, I told him when I set off for the station. He's always in and out, actually, except in the evening, for as I told you, he does lots of jobs for me, things I can't manage.'

'Doesn't he go out to work?' Holly asked curiously.

Her aunt hesitated, and looked as if she wished Holly hadn't asked. 'Well, no, not exactly.'

Holly sensed her reluctance, and became even more curious. They were passing quite near the other cottage now, and she asked more quietly: 'Is he old, retired perhaps?'

'Heavens, no!' her aunt seemed amused. 'He's only young. In his early thirties, I would say.'

The more she heard, the more Holly knew that this man was another scrounger. Something made her pause from saying any more. She was not her aunt's keeper. In a sense it was none of her business who Aunt Margaret let the cottage to. All the same, her interest was by now thoroughly aroused, and as they neared the barn she glanced back at the cottage. It was only small, two up and two down. A bright light shone out from the windows, blazing into the night defiantly, and she wondered about him. Perhaps *he* was dismayed, at a visitor arriving . . .

They set off with nine excited dogs, and even two of the stray cats ran about their feet as they struck upwards across heathery fields. The night was clear and starry after the rain, and the loch gleamed distantly, lit by the moon. Holly breathed deeply, feeling a small measure of content after the heartbreak and difficulties of the past few months. Her aunt had been right insisting that she came. Here she would be busy helping with the animals, and trying to forget the sadness that lingered after her mother's death, and the more recent harsh experience of finding that the boss's son really *did* believe he had the right to . . . she stopped and shivered, and her aunt's voice interrupted her thoughts as she called to one of the dogs who had ventured too far away. A few minutes later they turned and began to go down towards home.

Holly slept soundly that night, utterly exhausted after her long journey, and the sun was already high in the sky when she woke the following morning to find Bunty and Kitty curled snugly at the foot of the bed. She shooed them down, then went to wash and dress.

Everything was quiet when she went downstairs.

The three clocks, all showing slightly different times, as they had done for as long as she could remember, ticked noisily in the room, and Smokey and Kazan rose to greet her, but of her aunt there was no sign.

Thinking she might be in the barn, Holly went out and walked carefully across the yard, followed by the two dogs. She paused at the entrance to the barn to let her eyes adjust to the comparative gloom, and called: 'Aunty?'

There was silence, except for several dogs who roused themselves sufficiently to come and sniff her legs, their tails wagging. She walked into the large airy shed, curious to see what sort of work this man did. A framework of wood stretched many yards, and there was a wooden floor raised a foot or so from the ground, and supported by bricks. These were divided at intervals by hardboard panels, making self-contained kennels about four feet square. Although it was not finished, Holly could see that the workmanship was sound. The wood was neatly grooved, no nails showed, and already the dogs had made their beds on the thick piles of straw in each compartment. She bent to look more closely, and a voice from the door said:

'Mind you don't catch your dress. Some of that wood is rough.' The voice was deep and pleasant, and had an amused note to it. Slowly Holly straightened and looked round. A man was outlined in the doorway with the light behind him, and she couldn't see him clearly, only the tall broad-shouldered shape of him. Then he came forward, moving with an easy grace; a big man, perfectly at home, assured. He was dark, his face tanned and strong-featured. His eyes were dark upon her under their thick level brows, his mouth wide, well-shaped – and amused. There was a gipsy look about him, and she didn't like him. He was worse, far worse than she'd imagined, with an air of arrogant assurance about him as he surveyed her steadily from head to toe and back.

'I'm Gareth Nicholas. You're Miss Templeton's niece?' He held out his hand and Holly had no choice but to take it. His clasp was hard and firm like the rest of him, and she moved slightly away, instantly on the defensive, although she didn't know why, and that was annoying as well.

'I'm looking for my aunt,' she said. 'Do you know where she is?'

'She's not in the house?' One eyebrow lifted fractionally.

'No.' Holly didn't add, 'that's a stupid question', but it hung in the air just the same.

He stroked his chin reflectively. 'No,' he granted. 'Or you wouldn't be asking, would you?'

'I thought she might have come to see to the dogs.'

'She may have gone to the village—'

'But her car is still there—' she began.

'On her bike,' he finished smoothly. 'She often does in the morning. To the shops.'

Something stung Holly, she knew not what, perhaps his indolent, lazy, almost insolent assurance, and she said quickly, without thinking:

'I suppose she does your shopping too?' She regretted it almost instantly, but it was too late. Very slowly his eyes raked her face, and a gleam of something disturbing lit them as he answered softly:

'I'm not one of her lost dogs, Miss Templeton. I am perfectly capable of buying my own food as and when I need it. As a matter of fact your aunt enjoys cycling to the village. I've offered to take her several times in my Land-Rover when the weather is bad, but she prefers her independence, as I do.' He turned away abruptly, but before he went out, looked back and gave a curt nod. 'Good day, Miss Templeton.' Then he was gone. Holly ran her hand along the surface of the wood, oblivious to the dogs sniffing at her toes. He had been as quick on the attack as she had. She was uneasily aware that her hasty remark hadn't helped matters. Biting her lip, she wandered back to the house to make her breakfast, and as she did so, a horrible thought struck her. Supposing he had been in his back garden the previous night and overheard the conversation on the way to the barn? She had questioned her aunt about him then, about his going out to work, and he would have guessed her feelings by her tone. Perhaps he'd even seen her going into the barn just now, and wondered what *she* was like. The thought was vaguely disturbing, and Holly rubbed her hand quickly down her side as if to erase his touch. She had not liked him; she sensed that the feeling was mutual. There had been something in the way he had looked at her, a slight shrewd narrowing of his eyes, as if in assessment. Who did he think he was anyway? Holly looked at herself in the mirror over the sink, aware only of the heightened colour in her cheeks, oblivious of the beautiful dark eyes looking back at her, dark exciting eyes, with sooty lashes and thick shapely eyebrows above. She was unaware of her beauty, of the way her rich deep auburn hair shaped her face, of her own wide feminine mouth with its rich softness untouched by lipstick. She saw only that an arrogant, gipsyish stranger had made her feel small and very young. Idle layabout he might be – but he was certainly not one of the normal run.

Aunt Margaret returned later full of flustered explanations of why she was late. Holly silenced her with a hug. 'It's all right, Aunt, you mustn't hurry back for me, ever. I went into the barn to see if you were there, and Ga – Mr. Nicholas told me where you'd gone.'

She gave Holly a quick glance. 'Oh, so you've met him? Well, and what did you think of him, eh?' Her head slightly tilted, eyes twinkling, she regarded her niece curiously.

Holly shrugged, knowing she must be careful. 'Well,' she began, 'he's a bit different from what I expected. Younger, I think.'

'Hmm, not committing yourself. Still think he's a con-man, out to steal my jewels?'

Holly burst out laughing. 'Heavens, I never said *that*!'

Aunt Margaret patted her arm. 'I'm only joking, child! And you're only looking after your silly old aunt, I know. Personally,' and she began plumping cushions on a nearby chair, 'I think he's rather sweet. A bit eccentric, of course, but sweet.'

Holly's eyes widened. Eccentric! Sweet! Was this her aunt speaking? Her aunt went on: 'I'd like to have introduced you, just to see how he reacted. You're very attractive, Holly—' then as Holly made a deprecating gesture, 'No, don't look embarrassed, you are. That lovely auburn hair runs in the family.' She patted her own greying, untidy locks. 'You may not believe this now, but I used to be the belle of the ball when I was young – and you've got the same hair, and those dark hazel eyes, and thick lashes – why, you'd turn any man's head.'

Holly gave a little smile. 'Not at the moment – and certainly not *his*.'

Her aunt made a little face. 'You need a few nights' good sleep, that's all. That brute of a young man – you should have broken the vase over his head, impudent young puppy – where was I? Oh, yes, why do you say "not *him*" like that? You surely don't think there's anything – er – odd about Gareth?'

'I didn't mean that,' Holly interrupted hastily. No, there had certainly been nothing odd about him in one way. On the contrary, she had been made aware of a virile strength in those few unfortunate minutes in the barn, a kind of male awareness that at other, normal times might have set her pulses racing. He was a real man – and knew it. But there had been an abrupt shuttering of those enigmatic eyes – dark – what colour? With sudden shock, Holly realized that they were dark brown, almost black, an unusual colour. Now, she thought, why did I notice, I don't usually . . .

'I said you're miles away, child. Wake up! I'm away to make a pot of tea. I'm not as young as I was, and that hill back is steeper, I'll swear!' Muttering and shaking her head, puzzled at the ways of hills, her aunt went into the kitchen, and Holly followed carrying the handlebar basket crowded precariously with groceries.

When Holly offered to help her aunt insisted that she was to have a couple more days of idleness, to rest and grow strong. Holly, amused, said: 'And what have you in mind for me on Monday? A little light housework, perhaps?'

Her aunt's round cheery face creased with sudden laughter. 'Perhaps,' she admitted. 'I'll be glad of you, actually. It's lovely to have company again, and I don't do as much as I should in the house, what with the animals. Gareth will do anything I ask, of course, in fact he came and cleaned the entire house a couple of weeks ago, when I twisted my ankle. Did it as well as any woman too. *And* did all the shopping for a week.' She stopped abruptly, then added: 'You don't like him, do you?'

It would not have been fair – or possible – for Holly to tell her less than the truth. 'No,' she said. 'I don't.'

'Why, Holly?' Her round, open face was puzzled, almost anxious, and Holly hastened to tell her:

'It's just one of those mutual things – you know, it happens sometimes. You can meet a perfectly nice, ordinary person,' only he was neither nice nor ordinary, she thought inwardly, 'and bingo! all the vibrations are wrong, and there's nothing anyone can do about it.'

'Mmm, I know. Instant antagonism. It happens,' and she nodded sagely, measuring tea from the caddy into the pot, and Holly might have imagined her slight smile.

'Something like that.' She didn't add that she'd felt that strange prickling, the warning of danger, at the back of her neck when their hands had touched, because her aunt wouldn't have believed her, and suddenly she didn't want to talk about him any more.

Perhaps Aunt Margaret knew it, for she changed the subject, and Gareth wasn't mentioned again that morning.

Later, in the evening, Holly decided to go for a walk, and took Smokey, who bounded ahead woofing happily at this unexpected bonus as Holly donned mac and wellingtons. It was a fine clear night, and she walked a good way over the rough bleak heather-covered hills before deciding to return. It was nearly eleven as she scrambled down the last steep incline. For a moment she paused as a movement near Gareth's cottage caught her eye. Faintly a door closed, then a man's shape detached itself from the house and began walking down the track that led to the road. There was no mistaking, even in the pale moonlight, that broad-shouldered figure striding out silently on long legs. Where on earth, she wondered, was he going?

Her aunt looked up from the shapeless mass of knitting on her knee when Holly went in and asked her. 'I don't know. Of course, he comes and goes as he chooses,' she said. 'But I must admit it is a bit late. Did he see you?'

Holly shook her head. 'No. I was coming down the last stretch, and I was in shadow. In any case he didn't look back.'

'Well, I'll mention it tomorrow.' She broke off a piece of red wool, and began to put her knitting away.

'No, don't – I don't want him to think I'm spying on him,' Holly said hastily. Her aunt gave her an odd look, then chuckled.

'Heavens, I'm sure he wouldn't. Still, I won't, if you'd rather not.'

Soon afterwards they went to bed. Holly lay awake for ages, thinking of her mother, and her father, as she so often did, for the wounds hadn't yet completely healed. Only time could do that. When eventually she was about to fall asleep, she heard footsteps coming up the path, and went to the window.

Moonlight was behind him, elongating his shadow, making him seem almost sinister as he came quietly towards his cottage. As he neared, he looked up, and paused for a moment. Holly knew he had seen her.

She woke early the next morning, Sunday. Creeping

downstairs, she fed the kittens and let them out into the wire-enclosed run. A grey drizzle, giving everything a misty appearance, made them reluctant, but Holly was firm. She made a pot of tea, and took a cup up to her aunt, who lay in the huge fourposter that had been in the family for generations. Aunt Margaret stirred as she went in, blinked and yawned, then said sleepily: 'Good morning, dear.' Seeing the tea, she eased herself up. 'My, this is a surprise! But you're early, it's only—' she peered at the bedside clock, then gave up in disgust. 'Huh, no specs.'

'It's nearly eight, Aunt,' Holly told her, smiling. 'I thought I'd go to the kirk in the village. May I borrow your car? It's a grey morning.'

'Why, yes, the keys are in it, under the A.A. book in the glove compartment – it's a little temperamental in starting, though.'

'I'll manage, don't worry. Do you want any animals feeding before I go?'

Aunt Margaret sipped the hot tea appreciatively, grey hair awry, and looking so sweet and lovable that a lump came into Holly's throat. 'No, love, I'll get up soon. I know exactly how much to give whom. You get away now. There's a service at half past, you know.'

Holly stooped to kiss her aunt. 'I know. 'Bye.'

The Mini whirred a few times, then spluttered into silence. Holly bit back the unladylike word that threatened to come out, and tried again. This time there was a faint encouraging noise before that too puttered out. 'Damn, damn!' Holly sat back and looked round, wondering what to do next. At the following attempt the car juddered helpfully and willingly a few times, then collapsed exhausted. If she could push it, then get in quickly . . . No, if she missed, there would be one runaway car, and a lot of explaining to do.

She leaned over, about to lift the old umbrella from the back seat, when the passenger door opened and she turned round in relief to ask her aunt's advice . . . then took a deep breath as she saw Gareth Nicholas sliding in beside her.

'Having trouble?' he inquired cynically.

'It won't start,' she answered, moving imperceptibly away in the close confines of the small car. Clearly he had just got out of bed, and looked if anything, more gipsyish and disreputable than on the previous day. He wore a pair of old paint-spattered jeans, a navy blue sweater, and his face was covered with black stubble, making him seem darker than ever. Those amused sardonic eyes looked into Holly's. 'I gathered that. Let me try. Move over to this seat,' and he slid out and walked round the front.

He had the same result as Holly, then whistled softly. 'No go. I'll have a look later. Do you want a lift in the Land-Rover?'

'No, thank you.' Holly spoke stiffly, uncomfortably aware of his nearness. 'I'll walk. There's an umbrella here. I'll go and get a mac.'

'Where are you going?'

'To church in the village.'

'It's nearly two miles. You'll be soaked in this. Stay there, I'll not be a minute.' And he got out without waiting for her protest. Holly waited with mixed feelings, torn between reluctance at accepting any favours from this disturbing unpleasant man, and the knowledge that she would never walk it in time.

He came out pulling on an anorak, and ran to his Land-Rover behind the house.

Holly watched him driving it towards her, then ran

out and climbed in. 'Thank you, it's very kind of you,' she said.

He shrugged, concentrating on the rough track ahead of them, not looking at her. 'No trouble. Hold tight.' This as they came to a bumpy part of the rutted path. The rest of the journey was accomplished in silence, and Holly looked straight ahead wondering if the brittle atmosphere was entirely due to her over-working imagination, or if he felt it too. Her hands tightened on her bag and she tensed as, nearing the village, a dog ventured into the road, then thought better of it.

'Relax.' His voice was a soft intrusion, and she saw him glance at her legs, braced against the front of the vehicle. 'I wasn't going to run him over. Your aunt would never forgive me!' The mockery was there again, and she looked away out of the window without replying. A tight band lay across her chest, nearly stifling her. It had been a mistake to accept this lift. As they saw the tiny granite village kirk in the distance, already with several villagers making their slow mack-intosh-swathed way towards it, she said: 'You can drop me here, thanks.'

'I admit the transport leaves much to be desired, but I'm sure no one will mind,' he rejoined, and drove to the narrow gateway before stopping. He leaned over to open Holly's door, his anorak sleeve brushing her arm.

'Thank you again, Mr. Nicholas.' She was out, and closing the door before she gave in to the temptation to tell him what she thought of him.

'I'll walk home after.'

She didn't wait to hear his reply, if indeed there was one. She had never met a man like him before, one who could infuriate her in such a short time and with so few words. As she turned up the narrow overgrown path to the welcoming church, she thought back to what he had said. It was his manner more than the actual words, that was so infuriating. Almost as if he knew her feelings, and was doing his best to needle her, she thought. Yet there had been no need for him to offer her a lift. In a subtle way, she realized, he had succeeded in making her feel mean and ungrateful. Aunt Margaret thought highly of him, she knew. Perhaps, Holly reflected, as she stepped into the cool quietness of the little church, he was different with her. It would be interesting to see.

•

Holly stayed talking outside, in the shelter of huge old elms, with a few of the villagers when the service was over. Some had known her since childhood, and after telling them about her mother, hearing the sympathetic concern in their voices, she was a little upset. So many of them had known her father too, and the shadow of his death two years before was sometimes more bitter – because it had been so unnecessary.

She hadn't brought the umbrella, but carried a fold-away rainhat in her bag. Putting this on, she bade farewell to the softly-spoken Highlanders and set off walking home. The fine rain had intensified and it ran down her cheeks, mixing with the salt tears she couldn't stop.

She heard a vehicle pull up beside her and turned away, unwilling for anyone to see her. Then a voice, an all too familiar voice, said: 'Hop in,' and she turned reluctantly to face Gareth Nicholas holding the passenger door of the Land-Rover open, a little impatiently, it seemed.

Keeping her head slightly averted, she got in. 'You shouldn't—' she began.

'Your aunt asked me to meet you.' It was said with an air of finality that brooked no discussion, and she shivered down into her seat, a feeling of wretchedness overcoming all else. There was an implacable air of strength about him, and the hands that held the wheel as he drove swiftly along. If only she could have walked home . . .

'I should have phrased it better,' his voice cut in bleakly. 'Your aunt asked me, but I intended to come anyway.'

'Oh.' She was startled out of her mood. For a moment he'd seemed almost human.

'Thank you,' she said quietly. Perhaps he thought he had upset her!

They turned up the rough track from the road, and half-way up, almost in sight of the two cottages, he stopped. There was a moment's silence, then without looking at Holly, he said: 'Do you want to put on some make-up before you go in?'

She shook her head, and for the first time since getting in, looked at him. 'It doesn't matter,' she answered. 'Do – do I look awful?'

'No,' he smiled slightly, a mere quirk of the mouth. 'But I thought—' he shrugged and moved a lean brown hand to the gears. 'Sorry I mentioned it.'

'Don't apologize,' she said quickly. 'It was nice of you to suggest it.' She bit her lip, suddenly shy. 'I'm all right now.'

'Good.' He started off, and the Land-Rover slithered momentarily before getting a hold of the stones. Outside the house, Holly jumped out before he could open her door. 'Thank you for the ride,' she said.

He nodded, his manner as distant as before. The little interlude, when he had shown a rare thoughtfulness, might never have been 'You're welcome,' he said dryly. 'Any time.' But his eyes had gone cold and hard again, as blankly impersonal as a stranger's. Holly turned and walked slowly towards the cottage. She was obscurely frightened, but didn't know why.

After lunch Aunt Margaret asked Holly if she wanted to go with her to a farm several miles away, to take one of the dogs.

'But your car,' said Holly. 'It won't go.'

'Gareth fixed it,' her aunt looked at her, eyes twinkling. 'He knows all about engines. It only took him a few minutes. Something about sparking plugs,' and she waved a hand airily, presumably drawing them. Holly smiled. If her aunt had ever put her head under a bonnet, she would be most surprised. Things mechanical or electrical had always terrified her, and she therefore ignored them, on the principle that if she pretended they weren't there, they might leave her alone. Holly sometimes wondered how she had managed to cope, virtually single-handed, for so many years, yet amazingly she did. Aunt Margaret was one of those fortunate people whose cars only break down within yards of a garage; who find a policeman strolling past at the exact moment they discover they are lost in a strange city. Perhaps, thought Holly, it was something to do with her personality, the air of vibrant good humour and gentleness that she wore like a magic cloak. And I too, she thought, am drawn into this charmed circle, willingly, with love, and a deep respect that has lasted all my life. Her mind, as she neared seventy, was that of a youthful person, and she would never grow old, as people understood the word, Holly knew. She had been a teacher for years, and still coached one or two children, those with problems, or in need of extra tuition.

'I'd love to come with you,' Holly said. 'Which dog are we taking?'

'The one that looks like a sheep! He'll be marvellous with their children. They want him as a pet, of course,' she added, as Holly grinned. She knew how particular her aunt was about the homes the strays went to.

They set off a short time later. Gareth was coming out of his house as they got into the Mini, and Aunt Margaret called to him. He came over, and Holly watched, seeing no trace of the blank indifference on his face as he greeted the old woman. Head slightly inclined, he listened intently as she told him where they were going, and how long they would be. She was so small, she barely reached his chest, and he looked so tough and powerful standing there before her that Holly wondered again at the wisdom of her aunt in letting the cottage to him. She knew nothing about him, nothing at all, yet he had the freedom of her home. Yet how, thought Holly, can I make her see? She knows I dislike him – she'll think it's because of that.

They finished talking, and Holly heard him say: 'If you have any trouble with the car, phone from the farm. I'll come.' He gave her a small salute that might have included Holly, and opened the driver's door for her to get in. As they bumped down the track, Holly turned to reassure the huge dog shivering in the back seat, and she saw that Gareth was standing watching them.

'I didn't know that his cottage had a phone,' Holly

remarked, wondering if he ever wore anything other than sweaters and jeans.

'It hasn't, but he's fixed up an outside bell to mine – I'm sure it's illegal, but I can hear it if I'm in the barn, or outside.'

'So he just goes to answer it?'

'Well, yes, of course.'

'Oh, Aunty!' Holly sat back in despair, unhappily aware that this was one subject on which she and her aunt would never see eye to eye, and quite sure there was nothing she could do about it.

They reached the farm safely, stayed for a short while chatting and drinking tea with the farmer, a shy Highlander and his softly spoken wife, and their three young children. The youngest, a boy of six, John, was having difficulty at school and being teased by the others because he was a slow speaker and mover, and this tended to aggravate his problem.

As they left, the children out of earshot, Aunt Margaret said:

'If you want to bring John to me once a week, I'll see what I can do. There's nothing wrong with him – in fact, he's a very bright lad – and a little push in the right direction could work wonders.'

It was touching to see the mother's face light up. 'We would be very pleased,' she told Aunt Margaret shyly. 'John thinks very highly of you.'

'Then that's settled. Shall we say Tuesday, after school?'

Her aunt had a very satisfied look on her face going home, and Holly thought she knew why. 'You're an old schemer, aren't you?' she asked, watching her aunt's face.

Aunt Margaret laughed. 'Am I so transparent? I've

been itching to get my hands on him for a while. He'll surprise everybody one day, you mark my words. And I'm going to help him.'

'I didn't know you could be so crafty!' Holly shook her head in quiet wonder. Her aunt's chuckle was rich and infectious.

'Sometimes, yes, sometimes I am.' And something in the way she said it puzzled Holly. But she said no more.

CHAPTER TWO

THERE were two letters for Gareth delivered by the mail man the following morning. Holly took them into the barn, where her aunt was busy attending to the dogs.

'Shall I give Mr. Nicholas his letters, or push them through the door?' Holly asked her. Aunt Margaret looked up from the bucket of meat and meal that she was busy doling out.

'Oh, knock at the door, dear. I seem to remember he said he might be going into Strathmhor later today. Will you ask him, if he is going, if he'd fetch me some things back?'

'I'll ask him.' Holly hadn't been able to resist a good look at the envelopes before leaving the house, so that it was with no difficulty that she held them primly away from her now. One was typewritten, in a long white business envelope, the other was pale blue, from France, with his name and address in a very feminine scrawl – but no address on the reverse side, which fact perversely annoyed her. Ridiculous, because she knew it was no business of hers anyway.

She knocked firmly at the front door and heard him shout:

'Come in, it's not locked.' Reluctance fought with curiosity, and she pushed the door open into the tiny hall, with the stairs nearly on top of her. His voice floated downstairs: 'I'll not be a moment, Miss Templeton.' Clearly he thought she was her aunt.

'It's me, Mr. Nicholas. I've brought you two letters.

Shall I—' She stopped as he appeared at the top of the stairs.

'Well, well, what an honour! Good morning, Miss Templeton.' And he began walking slowly down the stairs towards Holly, a dry smile on his face. A sarcastic smile it seemed to her, and she felt her mouth tighten. He was insufferable! He was dressed in the same sweater and jeans that he had worn the previous day. Perhaps, she thought absurdly, he sleeps in them as well, to save time worrying about what to wear.

'Thanks.' He reached out for the letters, and Holly backed slightly, wishing a second later that she hadn't when she saw his sudden grin. 'The hall *is* rather small,' he remarked affably, 'isn't it? Still, it suits me. Won't you come in?' he gestured towards the kitchen. 'I mean, would you like a coffee? I'm about to make some.' An eyebrow lifted quizzically, as if he knew she would refuse.

'No, thanks. I'm just going to do the washing,' she answered, trying to smile pleasantly. 'I won't keep you. My aunt asked me to find out if you were going to Strathmhor later.'

'This afternoon, yes. Does she want me to bring something back?'

'Yes, please,' and she turned towards the door, but before she could open it, he reached out to do so himself. 'Allow me.'

'Thank you.' As she slipped through, his voice halted her.

'I'll call in later – and, Miss Templeton—'

'Yes, Mr. Nicholas?' she paused, embarrassed at the stilted formality.

'I wouldn't be in too much of a hurry to do the washing if I were you.'

'What do you mean?' She spun round ready to tell him to mind his own business. Who did he think he was?

'The washer was making a horrible noise last week and I promised to look at it, but forgot.' He gave her a slow, gentle, infuriating smile. 'So if you'll wait until I've had my coffee and toast, I'll be right over.'

'That's very kind of you – but don't get indigestion on my account. I'll find something else to do until you arrive. There are so many jobs in a house. Don't *you* find it so?' And she glanced quickly round, and gave him a faint smile.

The door was shut very firmly behind her. Good, she thought, I've managed to needle *him* now. Two can play at his game, she reflected as she went back to her aunt's house. She wondered again if he had overheard her words on the evening she had arrived. Short of asking him, she would probably never know.

She had to admire his skill with the washer. Much as she disliked the man himself, there was no denying that he had an efficient air about him as he knelt beside the machine, a box of tools beside him. Holly had gone into the kitchen to make a cup of tea, and Aunt Margaret was keeping well out of the way, on the principle that things worked better for her if she knew absolutely nothing about them. Gareth had come over less than ten minutes after Holly had left him, which fact gave her a small twinge of guilt. So that now, as she asked him if he wanted tea, she added: 'I'll make you something to eat as well, if you like.'

He looked up frowning, as if engrossed in his task. 'What? Oh, no, thanks. I'm not hungry.' And he bent again to fiddling with the intricate machinery. She squeezed past him, careful not to touch any tools, but he moved them anyway. 'That better?' he inquired dryly.

'I'm sorry. I didn't mean to get in your way.'

'You're not.' But a second later he swore softly under his breath as a screwdriver slipped, then grabbed his hand.

Holly looked round from filling the kettle at the sink, and her heart sank. It was her fault for disturbing his concentration, she was sure. She bit her lip. 'Have you hurt yourself?'

'It's nothing.' But as he took his other hand away, she saw the blood oozing out redly, and drew in her breath.

'I'll get the bandages,' she said, putting down the kettle, and she went quickly past him into the living-room for the first aid box. He was standing up when she returned, very tall and disturbingly masculine. It was most odd. Holly was quite used to putting bandages on, but her fingers seemed to be all thumbs as she measured off a length, then opened the antiseptic cream. The lint refused to be cut and she gritted her teeth. He stood perfectly still, watching, and she sensed the amusement in him as he said: 'Shall I?'

'I can manage,' she answered. He was so tall, she had to look up to reply, and something about the expression in his eyes was disconcerting to say the least. She bent hastily to her task again. A minute later the job was done, and he looked at his bandaged hand, moving the fingers experimentally.

'Thanks. You don't think I need a drop of whisky in that tea, do you?' he said, straight-faced. 'In case I feel faint or anything?' He was openly mocking now, clearly gaining some sort of satisfaction from Holly's discomfiture. It made her snap: 'You don't look faint to me!' She resisted the temptation to throw the first aid box at him. The man was a sadist! She moved away quickly, knowing that the worst thing she could do would be to let him see. She decided that the less she had to do with him, the better. That, though, was easier said than done, for when he came to the house after lunch, to get Aunt Margaret's shopping list, her aunt said, as if the idea had suddenly occurred to her: 'Don't you need anything from the shops, Holly? I'm sure Gareth would take you with him – wouldn't you, Gareth?'

He stood by the door, tall, indolent, completely at home in her aunt's house, and he nodded, 'Surely.' His dark eyes glinted with amusement.

Holly looked in panic at her aunt. Somehow she had managed to imply that Holly really wanted to go, but hadn't dared ask. 'But I – I don't—' she began, then stopped as Gareth lifted one eyebrow. That small expression was full of meaning, almost as if he'd said:

'Scared?'

There was quite a lot Holly wanted. She had barely any make-up or talc, she had packed so hurriedly. The temptation to refuse fought with his sly challenge, then as he said softly: 'I promise we won't be away long,' almost as if reading her mind, it decided her.

'Thank you. There are some things I need. I'll get my coat.'

As they set off down the long steep track, he looked at her briefly. 'Tell me,' he said in a pleasant conversational kind of tone that gave no warning of the shock of his words, 'do I really frighten you? Or do you just dislike men in general?'

The question jerked Holly upright in the seat beside

him. 'I haven't the faintest idea what you mean,' she answered icily.

'Oh, come off it,' he retorted. 'You know damn well what I mean. You look at me, most of the time, as if I'd just crawled out from under the nearest stone. And you shy away from me like a nervy kitten if I dare come too near.' Then as Holly drew in a deep breath, ready to do battle, he went on: 'Look at you now – bristling like one of those strays that's having its meal taken away.'

She put her hand out as if to open the door, furious, and he leaned across and slid the lock home. 'No, don't try and jump out. It would be a bit messy just here. Seen that ditch?'

'Then stop at once! I'm not sitting here to be insulted by *you*!' she breathed, feeling the hot colour flood her face. She fumbled for the lock, and he stopped abruptly, jerking her forward in her seat. His hand closed over her wrist, and he pulled it away from the door. 'Not so hasty. We're going to the shops, remember?'

'I'm not going anywhere with you, Mr. Nicholas – if that's your name,' she snapped. 'And take your hands off me at once.'

For answer he pulled her round so that she was forced to face him. Still holding her wrist, loosely, but with fingers like steel, he said quite softly: 'Calm down, little wild cat. Think – what would your aunt say if you went running back now?'

She relaxed slightly, knowing she had no choice. Clearly he had no intention of releasing her until he had had his say. Her chest heaved with the effort to keep still, and her mouth was set in a mutinous line as she said: 'All right, you've proved what a strong man you are. Just let me go – please.'

'That's better.' Slowly he eased his grip, then took his hand away. They were nearly a mile away from the cottages, almost at the main road, and short of an undignified struggle, which she had no intention of attempting, Holly must remain in the vehicle with him.

'You haven't answered my question yet.'

'I should have thought it obvious,' she retorted. 'No, I don't dislike *men*.' The emphasis wasn't lost on him. He gave a low whistle.

'Nasty! A bit below the belt, that. But then you women never fight fair, do you?'

'It depends how many women you've fought – and what kind,' she shot back, rubbing her wrist where his fingers had gripped. 'The kind of men *I* know don't fight women!'

He began to laugh. 'And sharp with your answers! Must be that rich red hair. You certainly have the temper to match it. So I can take it that this thing is strictly personal?' His eyes gleamed devilishly near.

'If you like.' She turned away to look out of the window.

'Ah, I see. Let me guess, then. Without wishing to be conceited, I don't think I'm all that repulsive to look at – so it must be the fact that I have no job, no ties, and in fact appear to be a thoroughgoing lazy slob. Is that it?'

She turned back to him. '*You* said it, not me. I just object to everyone playing on my aunt's good nature, that's all. She's too kind. She sees good in everyone – and you – you—' she stopped, unwilling to commit the final indiscretion of saying exactly what was in her mind, although the temptation was strong. He appeared to be able to read her thoughts, for he went on: 'And I am just trading on her good nature? Tell me, is it a seal of respectability for a man to have a nine-to-five job? I mean, if I set off every morning in pin-stripes and bowler, and came back in the evening with my briefcase bulging with sandwich papers, would *that* make me acceptable in your eyes?' His voice was mocking, even cynical, almost cruelly so, and Holly had the sensation of being overwhelmed by a stronger force than she knew how to deal with. She shook her head faintly, her hair brushing her cheek.

'No – yes – I don't know,' she answered, biting her lip. 'You're twisting my words around—'

'No,' he interrupted – almost gently, for him. 'It's you who are all mixed up. You already decided, even before you met me, what kind of man I was. And because I fitted that unconventional pattern you fell in the trap of believing you were right, and I was absolutely no good. Well, I'll tell you something, Miss Templeton, and you may believe it or not, as you choose. I have nothing but respect for your aunt, and for what she is doing with animals. My intentions towards her are strictly honourable. And by that, I mean that not only will I pay my rent regularly, but I have no wish to beg, steal or borrow anything from her. Do I make myself clear?' Then, as he bent to the gears again, he added: 'And I do happen to be called Gareth Nicholas.'

Holly took a deep breath. 'Have you finished?'

'Yes. Why? Is there anything else you wish to say?' He looked at her and his eyes were dark and hard, chips of ebony.

'Yes. I think you're insufferably arrogant!' she answered. 'Who – who the hell do you think you are!'

'I've already told you – Gareth Nicholas. I have another name, Francis – and even you must know who *he* was, so perhaps I have a right to be here, don't you agree?' and he laughed, a humourless sound that was the last straw. Holly turned on him, her hand going towards his face to wipe the mockery from it. Swiftly it was caught and held, and he shook his head. 'No, don't try. I have no intention of letting you smack my face. And if you did, you'd be sorry.'

'You'd hit me back?' she gasped. 'Yes, I can believe you would!'

'I didn't say so, but if you're so keen to find out, why not try?' And he released her hand and sat looking at her, challenging her with his eyes. Holly was suddenly frightened. What would he do, this unpredictable man?

'I wouldn't touch you,' she breathed. 'I wouldn't soil my hands.'

'You're an aggressive little spitfire, you know that? Quite a handful. Some poor fellow will have his work cut out taming you—'

'Well, it won't be *you*, that's for sure,' she shot back. He said nothing, merely gave her a steady stare, then started the engine. Holly sat beside him, seething, and they drove on to Strathmhor in silence.

In spite of the smouldering dislike between them, she managed to enjoy her brief shopping trip in the town, and met Gareth by the Land-Rover in the station car park. He glanced briefly at her parcels.

'Got everything?' he asked, in a disinterested tone. 'We'll go now. I did say we wouldn't be long.' And they drove home in complete silence.

A strange thing happened as they drove up the track. Aunt Margaret was standing at the cottage door, and as they bumped up the last few yards, she came out. It was disturbing to see the look of distress on her normally cheerful happy face, and both Gareth and Holly got out quickly and ran towards her.

'Aunt Margaret! What is it?' Holly caught her breath. 'Is it one of the animals?'

'No – yes, in a way. Oh, do come in, both of you.' She was nearly wringing her hands in despair, and Gareth and Holly exchanged glances in a temporary kind of truce as they followed her in.

She began right away, and even in the midst of her worry, Holly was relieved to see Smokey and Kazan in their usual places by the fire. They were all right . . .

'I've had a phone call from such a dreadful man,' she began. 'You know Major MacConnell's estate?' This with a look at Gareth, who nodded.

'It was sold recently to some new people. I've never met them, of course, but the man phoned just after you'd gone – a most impolite person. He said he'd caught two of the dogs damaging his flowers, and his gardener told him they belonged here, and that I ran some kind of boarding kennels.' She paused for breath, then sat down heavily on the chintz-covered settee. 'And he said – oh dear!'

'What? What did he say?' Holly knelt beside her. 'Tell us.'

'Well, he – I can't remember the exact words, but he implied that it was all highly illegal – me having all the strays like this, I mean, and he would put a stop to it.' She paused and looked at Gareth. 'What am I going to do?'

'First, where are the dogs?' He stood by the stone

fireplace, hands in pockets, an inquiring look on his face. 'Has he got them?'

'Yes, I think so. It's the two young ones. He'll probably have them tied up in a shed or something. Oh, dearie me!' Her mouth trembled, and Holly put a comforting arm round her.

'Don't worry, Aunt. I'll go and see him. He can't—'

'No, I'll go,' Gareth's voice cut in, and they both looked up. Something in his face silenced Holly even as she would have spoken, and he shook his head faintly. 'You'll rush in, and probably end up getting us all arrested!'

She jumped up. 'And what do you think you can do?'

Aunt Margaret looked up in puzzlement from one to the other, clearly aware of the tension between them, but not knowing why.

'I can fetch the dogs back, for a start. Then we'll see. It needs a calm approach. What's the man's name?'

'Colonel Radford, I think. Yes, it is. He's only lived there a few weeks, but I've heard in the village that he's an awkward customer. You don't think—'

'I don't think anything at the moment. Where does his land finish?' He seemed so calm, so unmoved by everything that was happening that Holly felt a surge of dislike go through her.

Her aunt, however, was visibly less tense, as though some of his unconcern was rubbing off on her. She stood up with an effort. 'I'll show you. We'll go out the back way.'

They followed her out into the vegetable garden that bordered on the thick dark pines. She pointed towards them. 'His land finishes in the wood. There should be a fence running through, but parts are missing, I know. That's why he's so annoyed, because they got in, but to say that I'm breaking the law—'

Gareth touched her arm. 'Don't concern yourself about that. Does he keep sheep?'

'Sheep?' Aunt Margaret looked confused, and Holly stared in amazement. What was he getting at? 'No, he's not a farmer, or anything like that. He has horses, I believe, and a couple of dogs. Perhaps he's afraid that his will be contaminated by ours! How—'

'Ssh!' Gareth leaned over her reassuringly, and Holly began, very reluctantly, to admire his complete command of the situation. 'Don't get upset, Miss Templeton. He's not going to do *anything* to you, I assure you. If he kept sheep, he would have a point. Even the nicest dogs can chase sheep, and do a lot of harm, but as he doesn't you've little to worry about. Now, I'm going to see him, and try and persuade him to repair his fences.'

Aunt Margaret looked at him, her eyes gently worried. 'Oh dear, are you sure—'

'Go and make yourself a cup of tea. I won't be long.'

'I'm going with you,' Holly said, starting to follow him as he strode round the back of the house towards his Land-Rover. He stopped so abruptly that she nearly cannoned into him. 'No, you're not. Stay here with your aunt,' and he looked coldly down at her, but she stood her ground.

'And if he refuses to give you the dogs back?' she demanded.

'Why should he? If he does, I'll phone the police at Strathmhor and have him up for dog stealing. It's as simple as that.'

'You heard my aunt. He's an awkward customer. Two of us can—'

'Listen. He's trying a bluff – and threatening an old lady. I don't like that.' And his face showed a ruthless hardness that lent truth to his words. 'I intend to be as civil as possible – but if he's as rude to me as he was to your aunt on the phone, I might be tempted to tell him a few home truths, and I'd hate to sully your lily white—' he looked closer, '—shell pink ears.'

'Don't be flippant!' Holly snapped, then realizing just how vulnerable was her position, added more gently: 'I'll sit in the Land-Rover, and not say a word.'

'You're very determined, aren't you?' He turned away, and she thought she'd lost, then suddenly he stopped. 'Come on. I'm a fool – but not a word. You understand?'

'Not a word.' She caught up with him. 'I just want to see him.'

He was silent on the journey down the road, and Holly sensed his preoccupation with the task ahead. She wondered how he would tackle this aggressive neighbour. She was soon to find out.

Colonel Radford's house was enormous, a great granite mansion that had been built in the days when spaciousness and elegance had combined – and money was no object. The mile-long drive was heavily tree lined, with huge rhododendron bushes banked sombrely, waiting for summer. Gareth drove up slowly; Holly wondered if he was regretting his offer to help, wondered too if he would be capable of speaking to this supposedly difficult man in the right way. Suppose he antagonized him even more? She gave him a swift sideways glance. She hadn't noticed before just how strong and determined his jaw was. His chin had a deep cleft, and jutted at a stubborn angle. His very appearance was enough to rouse the Colonel's ire, she imagined; roughly and casually dressed, always looking somehow as if he needed a shave, he was hardly calculated to impress someone who lived in a beautiful old house surrounded by acres of rich gardens. Yet she could not say anything. She didn't doubt that he would order her out of the Land-Rover if she dared to open her mouth. Holly sat back in her seat, determined to behave in such a way that he wouldn't find fault.

Then the house came into sight at last, and he gave a low appreciative whistle. He glanced at Holly. 'No wonder he's fussy!'

'Yes.' She nodded and decided to risk it. 'You won't – er—' She stopped as he began to laugh.

'Listen, I've already told you – fairly politely, I thought – to shut up. Just leave it all to me. Okay?'

'Yes. Yes, I will.' There was no time to say more, for they were drawing up to the house. Instead of stopping at the front he drove on round to the back, and stopped as the stables and various outbuildings came into sight. They were in a large cobbled yard. Nearby was a barn with a tractor outside, and a young man walked out, wearing overalls over a checked shirt. Gareth opened his door and jumped down, going towards him. The man waited, pitchfork in hand, a look of polite inquiry on his face. As Gareth drew near and spoke, the other pointed towards the house, then behind him, to one of the outbuildings. Holly couldn't hear the words, but the discussion seemed amicable enough, and she relaxed slightly.

Suddenly the young man turned and began walking towards the house, with Gareth by his side. Holly watched until they were out of sight, then sat back. She looked at the shed towards which the young man had gestured. Were the dogs in there? It seemed likely. It decided her. There was just time, if she hurried . . . As she ran quietly across the cobblestones she quickly suppressed a twinge of conscience. She hadn't promised not to *move*, only to keep quiet. She slid open the bolt, and two frightened young dogs hurtled out, nearly knocking her over in the joy of recognition. She bent to hold their collars, and a man's voice said, from somewhere behind her:

'Well now, and where did you spring from?'

She spun guiltily round to see the young man in overalls – and he was smiling. Limp with relief, she answered: 'I was waiting in the Land-Rover, and wondered if the dogs were in the shed.'

'And now you know?' He clicked his fingers, and both dogs sat. Holly looked from them to him, and back again, and he began to laugh.

'I've not been torturing them, you know. Only put them where they couldn't do any more damage for a while.'

'But the Colonel—' she began.

'Oh, his bark's worse than his bite – if you'll excuse the expression! He was pretty mad when he saw them tearing round the gardens, but I dare say he's cooled down now. I've just taken your friend in to see him.'

'Oh dear!' He looked puzzled at Holly's dismay, and she hastened to explain. 'I'm afraid he's annoyed with your employer, because he apparently threatened my aunt.'

'Oh, I see!' he gave a low whistle. 'So you're the old la – Miss Templeton's niece. Who's he – the boyfriend?'

'No!' Strangely she didn't resent the man's questions. He was in his mid-twenties, nearly as tall as Gareth, and as fair as the other was dark, with an open pleasant face, and nice smile. She sensed too his interest, not obvious, but there in the way he looked at her, with a wide understanding grin. 'You said that as if you meant it. Sorry I asked.'

'He rents a cottage from my aunt, that's all.'

'I see. By the way, I'm Mike.'

'Holly Templeton.' They shook hands, and his clasp lingered a fraction longer than strictly necessary as he said: 'Holly? What a fascinating name.'

She smiled. 'It's Henrietta really, but I couldn't say it properly when I was a baby, and that was how it came out, and—' she shrugged. 'Now I'm stuck with it.'

'Beautiful,' he murmured, and released her hand with reluctance. 'You know, you should have come on your own. You'd have had the old man telling you you could send all the dogs down here as often as you like.' He paused, then added: 'Does she really run an animal sanctuary?'

Suspicious of a trap, Holly said carefully: 'Well, she looks after a few strays, but it's not on a big scale, or anything like that. Just three or four.' She crossed her fingers at the fib, but it was in a good cause, and there was absolutely no need to mention cats *at all.*

His smile broadened. 'It's all right, *I* won't tell the old man. The less he knows the better. Besides, if you're coming out with me for dinner, I don't want to get on the wrong side of you.'

'What?' Her ears must be playing tricks. It seemed as if . . .

'I said, "if you're coming out with me for dinner", you will, won't you? I don't always dress like this, I promise. Please, Holly.'

He gave her a look of earnest pleading, and she smiled. He was nice. Not at all like someone else not so far away.

'Thank you, I'd like to,' she answered.

'Tonight?'

'No, not tonight. I must wash my hair—'

'Tomorrow?'

'All right. About eight?'

'I'll call for you at eight sharp. You know, I'm glad those dogs decided to stray, or I might never have met you, and – oh, oh, here's your friend.' They both turned and waited as Gareth came up and looked at the dogs, then at Holly. His face gave nothing away. He nodded to Mike. 'Everything sorted out, I think.' Then to her: 'Let's get them in the Land-Rover.'

After they were settled in, two rather subdued dogs sitting quietly in the back, Mike came to Holly's door and opened it a few inches. 'Till tomorrow, Holly.'

'Yes. Good-bye.' He watched them go, and Gareth said nothing until they were half-way down the drive, when Holly, unable to bear the heavy silence, said: 'How did you get on with the Colonel?'

'Never mind me. What the hell were you doing?' She looked quickly at him, surprised by something in his tone, and was amazed to see dark temper on his face.

'I – what do you mean?' she stammered.

'Don't look so damn pi-faced. I told you to stay put, and you promised. I should have known—'

'Just a minute! I promised to keep quiet, that's all. What am I supposed to do when someone speaks to me? Nod?' Her temper had flared to match his own, and he swept out of the drive, along the road for a few hundred yards, and stopped in a passing place, overhung by dark trees. Turning to her, he began: 'Don't split hairs with me. I should never have taken you. I turn my back for five minutes and you're dashing around making dates with young Radford—'

'Who?' What was he talking about? she wondered.

'Don't pretend. I heard him—'

'I don't mean that. He only works there—'

'Oh, yes?' his voice was heavy with sarcasm. 'With that Winchester accent? His name's Mike Radford, and he's the younger son of the esteemed Colonel. Don't tell me you didn't bother to find out his name before you made a date – or do you prefer it that way?'

'I don't have to take such rudeness from *you*!' she burst out. 'He introduced himself to me as Mike, that's all. What was I to think? I assumed he worked there.'

'I see. And you wouldn't have accepted if you'd known?'

Holly was silent. What could she say? She honestly didn't know. And she was puzzled and disturbed by Gareth's obvious anger. Had things gone badly in the house? She could hardly ask now. Mustering her wits, she said coldly: 'Hadn't we better be getting back home? My aunt will be worried. And just before we go I'd like to say one thing. It's no business of yours if I choose to go out with Mike, regardless of who he is. So there!' she finished childishly.

'It's my responsibility for taking you there in the first place.'

'I can look after myself,' she retorted. 'I'm eighteen, you know.'

'It's a pity you don't act it, then.' Savagely he started

the Land-Rover, and they drove swiftly homewards.

Aunt Margaret was again by the door, and Gareth strode over to her, leaving Holly to follow with the two dogs at her heels.

'Everything's fine,' he assured her as they all went into the house. Her face expressed disbelief and wonderment.

'You're sure? He's not—'

'No, he's not going to haul you into court. In fact, he's not half as bad as we imagined.'

'Tell me *everything*!' She rushed into the kitchen. 'I put the kettle on as soon as I saw the Land-Rover in the distance. I'll make you tea. You must need it, dear boy.' She was fussing round him like a mother hen, great relief lighting her plump features as she popped her head round from the kitchen. He followed her to the door, and Holly stood in the living-room, knowing she might as well not have been there. She watched him as he spoke, and there was something about him, about the way he stood, the expression on that dark gipsy face, that she didn't understand.

'I saw the son first, and he took me to his father. The Colonel was rather—' he hesitated '—brusque at first, but we were soon talking. He asked me to apologize for his manner on the phone, by the way. He'd just caught the dogs rolling round in his favourite rose bed, and was, in his own words, "hopping mad". Once he'd locked them up and phoned, he checked the damage, and it wasn't too bad. I offered to replace any rose bushes, but he wouldn't hear of it,' he paused, then added in a very puzzling way: 'We parted on the best of terms.'

'Oh, I'm so glad,' Aunt Margaret breathed. 'I do so dislike unpleasantness. But the fences, what about them? I'm frightened that this will happen again.'

'He'd not realized they were in bad repair. He's had a lot to do, but he'll get his son – Mike, I believe his name is—' this with the merest flicker of a cool glance towards Holly, '—to check them.'

'Gareth, my dear, what can I say? You are truly marvellous. I would have been so upset if only Holly and I had been here—'

'I think your niece would have coped admirably, Miss Templeton. As I say, he wasn't as bad as I thought, and in fact—' and he stopped.

'Yes? What is it?'

'Well, he's invited the three of us to dinner on Saturday night.'

'What?' Both Holly and her aunt said it together.

He nodded apologetically. 'It's true. I said I felt sure you'd both be delighted. Did I do right?' He looked from her to Holly, and she detected the faintest gleam of mockery in his eyes as they met hers.

'Well! I'm too startled to think straight, but of course, it would have been very bad form to refuse. My word! It's unbelievable. One minute threats, the next an invitation to dinner.' Aunt Margaret filled the teapot hastily. 'I think I need a drink more than you now. Oh, dear, what shall I wear?'

But Holly watched him, and said nothing. There was something here that she didn't begin to understand. Colonel Radford couldn't have changed *so* much in the space of a quarter of an hour – yet he had. What on earth could have made him invite this arrogant, infinitely puzzling man to his house? The whole situation began to take on a dreamlike quality, as if it weren't really happening. One more thing she found mystifying. If, as Gareth said, everything had gone so well, why had he been annoyed at her accepting the son's dinner invitation? It didn't make sense, not at all. Nor did the look of secret knowledge, a look that Holly glimpsed before he wiped it from his face.

CHAPTER THREE

HOLLY was busily trying to weed the overgrown front garden the next afternoon when she heard a van making its laborious way up the steep track, and she looked around. She had forgotten all about the new pupil, and watched him get out and wait for a moment on the path until his father joined him. Aunt Margaret came out to greet them.

'Come on in, John,' she called. 'And you, Mr. MacDonald, will you come in for a cup of tea?'

'Ach, no, I'll away now, if ye do not mind. But I'll be back for the lad in an hour. Will that be all right with you?'

'That will do nicely.' She took the shy, frightened-looking boy's hand. 'I have some books waiting for you inside. Good-bye, Mr. MacDonald.'

Holly was seeing a different side to her aunt. Gone was the gentle air of inefficiency; in its place was a brisk capable manner as she walked into the house with the nervous little boy, and closed the door behind them. If anyone can help John, Holly thought, it will be you.

She looked across to Gareth's cottage, wondering where he was. She had seen him go out a few hours previously, and he still hadn't returned. And late last evening, he had gone out walking again; it had been raining heavily, but that was clearly no deterrent. She had seen him setting off, dressed in anorak, his trousers tucked into thick wellingtons. He hadn't returned for over two hours. She was annoyed with herself for her curiosity, but had found sleep strangely elusive until the faint squelching footsteps had come up the muddy track. She hadn't gone to the window for fear he would see her. But she had listened, and when his door closed quietly, she had fallen asleep.

Before lunch he had come in to ask Aunt Margaret if she needed anything doing before he went out, and at her refusal, had left. He hadn't asked Holly – but that was hardly to be wondered at. The atmosphere was brittle with tension whenever they were in the same room. She still smarted from his arrogant remarks the previous day. She hadn't known who Mike was – but he didn't believe her. She bent to her weeding again, glad of a form of release from the explosive energy within her. Kazan bounded up, wanting to play, then woofed and began wagging his tail as the distant but distinctive note of the Land-Rover's engine was heard. Holly's mouth tightened rebelliously. So he was coming back, was he? She determined not to speak – then had no choice, for as he arrived and got out, he began walking purposefully towards the cottage.

Holly stood up. 'Mr. Nicholas?' He paused, then turned slowly round as Kazan bounded towards him with enthusiastic yelps.

'Yes? You want me?' The merest trace of a grin accompanied the words.

'No! But perhaps I'd better tell you. My aunt has a pupil with her. Unless it's urgent, I don't think she'll want disturbing.'

'I see.' He walked slowly towards her, hands in pockets, moving quietly and easily. 'It's nothing that can't wait.' And his eyes watched Holly, taking in every detail of the old jeans and sweater that she wore in an insolent appraisal. 'I'll call in to see her later.' He had changed his sweater, she noticed. Now he wore a chunky Aran one in oatmeal colour. It emphasized the breadth of his powerful shoulders, and his tan, making him look almost foreign, a dark stranger that she disliked intensely. Yet there was something about him that was physically attractive, she had to admit – reluctantly. The tough aggressive air was still there, but not for the first time, Holly sensed another side to his puzzling character. A deeper thread of quiet strength had shown itself the previous day, when he had heard her aunt's distress. There was nothing soft about this man, and yet for a while, she had seen genuine concern on that teak-hard face, concern for an elderly woman who was being bullied – and an immediate desire to do something about it. As indeed he had – only too efficiently, it seemed. Perhaps, Holly mused, he wasn't as hopeless as she had thought, for he possessed the true desire of the strong to protect the weak. Suddenly embarrassed, as if he might read her thoughts – something he seemed to have an uncanny ability to do – she bent to he task again, wishing he would go away.

He didn't. After watching her for a moment, he said: 'You really should wear gloves for that job,' and as she looked up surprised at his concern, he added: 'It might spoil the effect tonight if your hands are grimy.' And he smiled as he turned away.

Holly glared at the broad retreating back, lost for words, then threw a huge clump of docks into the plastic bucket beside her, resisting the strong temptation to fling it at him instead. Insufferable man! She looked ruefully at her hands. He had a point there. They would need a good scrub before her date with Mike.

She heard the door click decisively behind him, and pulled her tongue out – childish, she knew, but satisfying. How on earth had he charmed Colonel Radford sufficiently to wangle a dinner invitation from him? And would Gareth go dressed as he usually was? She giggled at the thought. It would be interesting to see.

Holly was ready at a quarter to eight for her date that evening, and went downstairs to her aunt. She wore a white trouser suit in heavy dacron, with the faintest thread of silver running through. It was her favourite, and she knew it suited her. Yet she didn't know just how startlingly attractive she was, however, her slender figure graceful in the clinging material, her fair skin glowing from her exertion in the garden, and her short hair curling round her face, framing it to perfection, emphasizing the classical bone structure and delicate lines of cheek and forehead. She wore a little make-up so that the scattering of freckles on her nose and cheeks were hidden. She hated them, but had had them all her life, and knew that after an hour in a warm room they would emerge, as they always did.

'Oh, Holly, you look simply lovely!' Her aunt watched her with hands clasped to her ample bosom. 'Do let me lend you the amber pendant – it will match the lights in your hair.'

Holly shook her head. 'Honestly, I'd rather not. It's too valuable. I'd be frightened of losing it.'

'Nonsense! I never wear it now – and it cries out to be worn. I insist.' And she produced it with a flourish from the fruit bowl on the sideboard, proving what Holly already suspected; that she'd had it ready.

'Thank you.' She went and hugged her aunt, who said anxiously:

'Mind now, don't spoil your make-up! You look so sweet, my dear. I hope you'll enjoy your evening.' She had been only mildly surprised when Holly had told her that the Colonel's son had asked her out to dinner.

Now she carefully fastened the heavy gold pendant round Holly's neck. The large heart-shaped piece of amber glowed warmly in the light, rich in its gold setting, and infinitely beautiful. She knew instantly that this was the finishing touch her suit had lacked. As Holly touched its heavy smoothness, a knock came at the front door.

Aunt Margaret looked at her. 'That'll be him, dear. Go on, let the young man in.' Holly went and opened the door – and saw Gareth standing there.

'Oh! Come in.' She stood aside, and he entered. His eyes flickered briefly over her, lingering, she noticed, on her hands. Holly thrust them out. 'I scrubbed hard,' she told him. He wasn't a whit embarrassed – but what had she expected? she thought breathlessly.

'So I see. You look very nice.' He inclined his head slightly as he said it, and there seemed to be no trace of the usual sarcasm in his voice.

'Thank you.'

Aunt Margaret came forward. 'Did you want me, Gareth?' She was well aware of their mutual antagonism, had in fact commented on it earlier, and now she seemed determined that they wouldn't argue.

'Yes. I was in Inverness today and found a shop where they sell enormous quantities of dog meal cheaply. I bought a twenty-eight-pound sack. Did I do right?'

'Yes, of course. We'll sort it out on rent day. Where is it?'

'You were busy when I came back, so I've left it in the Land-Rover – but I'll fetch it in, or put it in the barn, whichever you like.'

Holly looked at one of the clocks, which said eight o'clock. The suspicion that he had come deliberately just as she was about to go out grew in her mind. He didn't normally appear in the evenings, her aunt had said, but now as he stood there, indolent, assured, he seemed to have no intention of leaving. She tensed as she heard a motor coming nearer, and looked briefly at him. He caught the look, and returned a dark level glance of his own. 'That sound like your escort,' he remarked affably.

'Yes, it does.' She leaned over to pick up her handbag from the settee, and he reached out and passed it to her. 'The path's rather muddy outside,' he commented. 'Mind you don't splash your suit.'

'I'll try not to,' then to her aunt: 'I won't be late.'

'No, dear. You'll stay and have a cup of coffee, Gareth?'

'I'd like to. Thank you.' There was a knock at the door, and as Gareth was nearest, he opened it. Mike stood there, looking very attractive in grey suede jacket and slacks.

'Do come in,' called Aunt Margaret, and her hand went to her hair as if to tidy it.

Holly introduced them, and Mike, after the polite 'how d'you do's' said: 'I'm very pleased to meet you, Miss Templeton. I believe you're all coming to dinner on Saturday?'

'Yes, my dear.' She was clearly impressed with this charming young man with his pleasant attractive face.

'My father told me to ask you to come about seven, if that's agreeable, to have drinks first.'

'Why, yes. Thank him very much. I mustn't stay late, of course, because of the animals, you know, so seven will be lovely.'

'That's settled, then.' He seemed relieved. 'Shall we go, Holly? You look marvellous.'

Then they were outside, and he remarked, as he helped her into the sleek white Jaguar that waited: 'I must have known what colour you'd be wearing.'

Holly laughed as he started the engine. 'You mean you have a car to match every outfit?'

He grinned. 'Not exactly. But we've got a maroon Jag as well. I nearly came in that.'

She pretended to shudder. 'Sorry I can't oblige. That's a shade that's fine for cars, but—'

'I know. I was kidding. Seriously though, Holly, you look absolutely super. We're going to a little place I know, about thirty miles away. They do a marvellous meal, and we can dance afterwards. Does that sound all right for Madame?'

'It sounds fine, Mike. Thank you.' She was surprised to find how relaxed she was with him, even though she scarcely knew him. She settled back comfortably as the powerful car purred smoothly along, swallowing the miles with no effort. The 'little place' turned out to be a huge hotel in the middle of a pine forest up in the hills towards Inverness, with dozens of cars parked along its wide drive. Music came faintly from inside, and light blazed out from the many tall windows.

'Little?' murmured Holly faintly.

Mike laughed and took her hand as she got out. 'Come on, I want to show you off. Why did you cover up those gorgeous freckles?'

She looked at him, startled, one hand flying to her face.

'Why do you think I asked you out? Can't resist freckles, and when I saw you standing in the yard—'

'That reminds me,' she interrupted, halting her steps. 'You got me here under false pretences—'

'Oh oh! All right, I own up. But let's face it, if you'd known who I was, would you have accepted?' Then, seeing her doubtful expression, he added: 'I didn't tell any lies anyway. I merely omitted to mention my surname.'

'Yes, but—'

'Yes but nothing! I know what my old man can be like. Can't understand how that fierce boy-friend of yours had him eating out of his hand so soon, though.'

'He's *not* my boy—' she began indignantly, and Mike silenced her with a squeeze of his hand.

'Sorry! I'm glad he's not, anyway. Never trust a dark man like that!'

Something struck Holly. 'What do you mean, he had him eating out of his hand?'

He lifted a cynical eyebrow. 'Well, when I took Gareth in I had visions of a speedy punch-up – which is why I retired gracefully back to the yard – and incidentally, found you. The old man, my dad, I mean, has a temper like nobody's business, but when I went back in, after you'd gone home with the dogs, he was as sweet as sugar. Wouldn't say why, except that your Gareth was a "grand young feller". I quote his exact words.'

'I don't believe it!'

'Neither did I, but it's true, I swear.' They had reached the main door, up imposing stone steps, and he opened the door for Holly.

After that, there was really no chance to talk, for they were greeted immediately by a group of young people, all obviously 'county', casually and elegantly dressed, and introductions followed, and Holly concentrated on remembering the names to fit the faces. Charles – Ian – Helen – Fiona – Douglas . . . Everything was a whirl of sound and colour and smiling young faces as they laughed and talked, and she gradually lost her first shyness and began to enjoy herself.

The drink flowed freely, and the meal was superb, and afterwards they danced. By eleven-thirty, Holly's head was reeling with the unaccustomed drinking she had done, and it was almost a relief when Mike whispered: 'I'm going to take you home. I don't want to make a bad impression with your aunt on our first date.'

'Can we go? I'm enjoying myself immensely, but—' She paused, and blinked.

'I know. You're not really used to it, right?'

She nodded, and he took her hand. They said goodbye to the rest of the crowd, and went outside. A few minutes later they were on their way home.

Mike stopped the car outside the front door, reversed it ready to leave, then took hold of Holly very gently, and kissed her.

'Thanks for a lovely evening,' he whispered, as his lips brushed her cheek. 'Can we do it again – soon?'

Holly was taken by surprise with the kiss, and moved slightly away. 'I've enjoyed it very much, Mike, and thank *you* for a wonderful time. And I'd love to go out again. Phone me?'

'I will. Good night, Holly.'

She waited in the porch and waved him off. Then, smiling slightly to herself, she went in. The orange-shaded lamp glowed in the corner, and she slipped off her shoes with a sigh of relief. 'Ah, that's better!' She rubbed her left foot gently. A long lean figure uncurled itself from the settee, and Holly, startled, dropped her shoes.

'What are you doing here?' she gasped.

Gareth stretched lazily. 'That's a nice way to greet me after I waited up for you! Want a coffee?'

She ignored the question, obscurely angry. 'I didn't ask you to!' she retorted.

'No. But your aunt and I were talking, and time passed, and after we'd taken the dogs out I could see she was tired, and said I'd go home.' His dark eyes, shadowed in the dim light, held hers in that disconcertingly steady gaze. 'And she said no, she wanted to wait up until you came home safely, so—' he shrugged indolently, 'I volunteered. I found a book, and sent her off to bed.'

'There was no need—' she began stiffly.

'Perhaps not. But she thought there was. After all, you are only eighteen, and this – er – Mike is virtually a stranger, isn't he?'

Coming from him, that seemed rich. Holly controlled the retort that sprang to her lips and said: 'Maybe, but his manners are perfect, I assure you.'

There came that infuriating lift of one dark eyebrow, highly amused. 'Oh, undoubtedly. And I'm sure his pedigree is equally immaculate.' There was no doubt about it, he was laughing at her.

'Is that supposed to mean something?' she asked sharply.

'Why, no!' He seemed surprised. 'Just a comment in passing. As one of the gentry, he's quite suitable as an escort.'

'I find your remarks very offensive,' retorted Holly. 'And let me remind you, I didn't know who he was when I accepted the invitation, so that fact hardly applies.' The drink was doing strange things to her, and she felt remarkably lightheaded.

'Ah, no, of course. I forgot that.' But the dry smile belied his words.

'You don't believe me, do you?' she challenged him, suppressing a hiccup. Their eyes met, and she felt the deep strength of his puzzling personality as he answered softly, never taking his eyes from her: 'I would never call a lady a liar.'

'You surprise me,' she answered swiftly. There was in her some urge to defy the complete control he was assuming, as if she needed to fight this stranger. She had never met anyone like him before. And yet there was something exhilarating in the conflict; some tangible tension that vibrated in the room like electricity. She sensed that he too was aware of it.

He nodded. 'You're wasting your time with him, you know,' he remarked.

'Mind your own business!' Holly snapped. She was trying hard to keep calm, but it was difficult.

'Of course I will – but I thought you ought to know. He'll never do for you. Not strong enough, you see. A nice enough boy, I imagine, but too – what shall I say? – too pliable. You'll find him agreeing with you, just to keep the peace, and then, after a while, you'll despise him.'

'Will you *get out* of here?' She went over to him, furious, and that was a mistake she discovered immediately, for without her shoes he was so much taller that she felt ridiculously small.

He looked down at her, and he knew. A slow smile of pure enjoyment broke on his face. 'You really do look pretty when you're hopping mad,' he said. 'A little red-haired spitfire. What a combination – freckles and a carrot top! Dynamic!'

Completely insensed, her head tingling with drink – and with his insolence – Holly swung her arm up and hit him across the face with a resounding slap. There was deadly silence for a few seconds.

'You've been itching to swipe me ever since we met, haven't you?' His words broke the silence, and something about them should have warned her, but didn't.

'Yes, I have!' She stood her ground and glared at him, uncomfortably aware that her legs had suddenly gone rather shaky.

'Well, don't say you weren't warned when you tried it last time,' he said, and suddenly pulled her towards him. She struggled vainly and the faint male scent of him was about her as his mouth crushed hers into submission for a few smouldering moments of time. Then just as abruptly, he released her, keeping his hands tightly on her arms as he said: 'And how do you like that?'

'Let me go! You – you—' A pulse throbbed in her throat.

'Ah-ah! No swearing. Ladies don't swear.' The dark gipsy face was taunting in its nearness. 'That's a fair exchange, I think. Try hitting me again and the same thing will happen. Now, if I let you go, will you behave?'

'No – yes, I – you're horrible you *beast*!' she ground out furiously. He dropped his hands away from her arms, and she rubbed them, weak and trembling with reaction. 'Go away!'

'Don't worry, I'm going. I'll have coffee at home. I wouldn't trust you not to lace it with arsenic. So long, little wildcat.' He tapped her chin lightly, and she knocked his hand away. and heard him laugh as he walked out of the house. Holly put her hand to her mouth, as if to erase the touch of his lips. Hers burned like fire. No one had ever kissed her like that before. How she hated him!

The next few days passed swiftly, and the weather, for late October, was mild and pleasant. Holly was kept busy in the garden or house, and so too was Gareth, for she saw little of him. When it was unavoidable, she was coldly polite, while he for his part seemed astonishingly amiable. Even her aunt remarked on it.

They were in the barn on Saturday, sweeping out and cleaning. Gareth had finished the dogs' kennels, and everything was very businesslike. Aunt Margaret chuckled. 'I hope the Colonel doesn't see in here,' she confided. 'He'd never believe I just had occasional strays.'

'I wouldn't worry about him,' Holly answered. 'Gareth seems to have well and truly sorted him out.'

'Mmm, yes.' She gave her niece an odd look, then said quickly: 'Strange, isn't it? I wonder what he's like? I'm going into the village this afternoon to have my hair done by old Mrs. Macrae. Gareth said he'd run me.'

'He might persuade her to cut his hair while he's there, then,' Holly remarked. 'He could do with it.'

'Oh dear, I do hope you'll be nice to him this evening.' Aunt Margaret looked worriedly at Holly, who laughed.

'Don't worry, of course I will. I'll be the perfect lady, I assure you. Besides, Mike will be there. He told me when he phoned me yesterday that it should be a good evening. His father's pulling all the stops out.'

'You know, I can't understand why you dislike Gareth so.' She turned a puzzled face towards Holly, and rested her hands on the broom. 'He can be perfectly charming.'

'To you perhaps,' Holly said. 'Which is as it should be. Don't worry about me.'

'But I want you to get on well. And you can't say he's been rude to you at all these last few days. Er – you didn't have an argument at all that night he waited up did you?'

'Not exactly,' Holly said dryly. 'Just a slight difference of opinion, you could call it.' She smiled at her aunt. 'Don't worry, we're poles apart, that's all. It happens all the time.'

'Mmm, I wonder? He's a Scorpio, of course, that might explain it.'

'Scorpio?' For a moment Holly didn't understand her, then realized. 'Oh, Aunt! Are you still interested in astrology?'

'Of course!' She looked faintly indignant. 'It's very important. I'll bet we find the Colonel is also one of the water signs – Pisces or Cancer – which should explain why they got on so well.'

'Don't forget I'm Pisces,' Holly said. 'So it hardly follows. But why do you say it so definitely? There's nothing in it, is there? And how do you know he's Scorpio anyway?'

'I knew it as soon as I saw him, so I asked him, and he told me. Seemed a bit startled. But it was obvious he's a true Scorpio character, dark and strong, very deep personality – a bit secretive, I imagine.'

Despite herself, Holly was intrigued. 'He's that all right,' she agreed. 'We know nothing about him, do we?'

Her aunt seemed not to hear that. 'You know, I forgot about you being Pisces – how very fascinating!'

'Aunty, really! If you have any ideas—' Holly began, and then stopped as footsteps sounded outside. Gareth came just in the doorway, and stopped. 'I thought I heard voices,' he said, and smiled. Just what had he overheard? 'I wondered what time you wanted to go to Kishard,' he said. 'And I'll be ready.' Then with a look at Holly: 'Do you want to go as well?'

'No, thanks.' For the benefit of her aunt, Holly gave him a nice smile as she said it.

'Fine,' he nodded, not really caring.

'I said I'd be there about two, Gareth, but old Mrs. Macrae's never bothered about time. You'll have lunch with us first. I've a chicken on. It'll be ready at one.'

'That's very kind of you, Miss Templeton. Thank you.' He turned as if to go. 'I'll be over at one. I have some work to do now.'

Holly waited until his footsteps had died away, then asked her aunt: 'Have you been in the house since he came?'

'Yes, once or twice. Why do you ask?'

'I just wondered. What does he *do*? I mean, he must have some hobby. He can't just sit there all day and every day at the times he's not helping you.'

'Oh, I don't know, dear.' She looked slightly shocked, as if Holly shouldn't have asked. 'I've only been in the kitchen, as a matter of fact. I took him some home-made cake over one day, and he ushered me straight in there. I certainly didn't go peeping in the other room. Perhaps he reads – I do know he has a lot of books – he might be studying for something. Yes, that will be it. He's very intelligent, you know.' And she seemed relieved at finding a suitable solution for the problem of Gareth's leisure activities.

Holly left the subject alone, but she was still curious. She felt too that if she knew, it might help her understand the puzzling, disturbing man a little better. But she couldn't foresee what a shock it would be when she did find out.

After lunch, Holly had a leisurely bath while her aunt and Gareth were away. As she lay back in the warm scented water, she looked ahead to the evening before her. How would it go? Aunt Margaret would enjoy herself, Holly felt sure. She had the ability to gather people round her, and Holly felt certain that even the irascible Colonel, that unknown factor, would succumb to her aunt's magic charm. Mike would be pleasant and polite, she knew. And that left Gareth. At the thought of him, Holly's heart beat faster. He didn't seem to like Mike – completely without reason – and yet he had apparently won over Mike's father. How would he be tonight? How would he fit in with the completely different atmosphere of a country house? There was no way of knowing in advance.

As Holly soaped herself, her skin pink and glowing with warmth, she realized, with almost a shock, that she was very interested in seeing how Gareth would look when they went. She stepped out at last, annoyed with herself for such childish curiosity. What did it matter? *He* wasn't important, not at all. Yet even as she thought it, she knew she was trying to deceive herself. In a way, the success or failure of the evening depended on him. It was through him, and his meeting with the Colonel, that they had been invited. In a sense, he would be the key factor of the entire evening.

Holly dried herself and slipped on a kaftan, one her aunt had insisted on her having – as it was, 'much too long, and much too tight for her'. Holly suspected it had been bought with her in mind, though Aunt Margaret would never admit it. It was warm and comfortable, a rich blue, floor-length, beautifully embroidered, and made her feel like a princess.

She heard their return as she was feeding the kittens in the kitchen. They had grown tremendously in a week, and had a tendency to wander all over the house, with resultant puddles on all the carpets, if not checked. Holly wondered how many more strays would arrive. Aunt Margaret had already found good homes in Kishard for three of the kittens, when they were old enough to go, and a dog.

The front door opened and she called out: 'I'm in here,' expecting her aunt to be alone. But it was Gareth who came in, carrying a large box of groceries which he put down on the table.

'Your aunt's at the front,' he said, 'talking to the policeman from Strathmhor.'

'What!' Holly gasped, and straightened up quickly, nearly knocking over a saucer of milk. There was only one policeman for sixty miles. It must be something serious to bring Sergeant MacLeish here. Could the Colonel . . .

'Don't panic. Nothing's wrong. Only—' he seemed to be having difficulty keeping his face straight '—I think she's about to take on a new lodger.'

Holly shot him a suspicious glance. 'What do you mean?'

'Well, his son found a huge Afghan hound straying in the main street of Strathmhor, and no one seems to know anything about it. I think he's trying to persuade her to mind it. We overtook them on the way back here, and he signalled us to stop. I thought for a minute I'd missed a radar speed trap.'

She ignored this attempt at humour. 'I'll go and see—' she began.

'Like that?' He gave a twisted grin, and looked lingeringly at the kaftan.

She pulled it closer round her. 'I'm quite respectable, which is—' and she stopped.

'Which is more than you can say about some people?' he suggested. 'Why don't you say it? Frightened of me?'

'No. I don't intend to argue, that's all. If you'll excuse me?' She made as if to pass him, but he didn't move.

'Not yet,' he said softly. 'There's nothing *you* can do.'

'I was going upstairs for something,' she retorted. '*If* you don't mind.'

'You haven't finished feeding these poor devils yet,' he answered, and bent to pick up a more adventurous kitten who was now trying to climb the leg of the kitchen stool. 'You know, I might have one of these myself,' he said, as it purred violently and began trying to unravel his thick dark sweater with tiny needle-like claws. He disengaged them gently, and Holly looked at him with something like horror on her face.

'You can't,' she burst out. 'It wouldn't be right.'

'Right? Why not?'

'You – you'll move on, won't you – and what then?'

'I don't understand you.' His voice was flat and hard. 'What makes you think I'll be "moving on", as you put it?' His eyes were very dark, and seemed to hold Holly as if mesmerizing her.

How could she answer what was in her heart? That he seemed to her a nomad, unable to settle anywhere? She shook her head, unable to speak, for an under-current was in the air, one she scarcely understood, but it made her nervous. Not for the first time, she was uneasily aware of the effect he had on her just by being there. It was quite absurd, she knew. She wasn't frightened of him – yet in a way she was. Even as she admitted it to herself, he laughed, low, and amused. 'Trimmed your claws since Tuesday?' he asked. 'Lost a little of the fire? Shame!'

Holly's cheeks reddened. He really was the most annoying man – and seemingly a mind-reader, that was the disconcerting thing.

'If you must put it so crudely,' she answered, 'yes, perhaps I have. I just don't think anyone should have an animal unless they can give it a settled home.'

He nodded. 'I see. And now I'll tell you something. I like it here. I'm going to stay – and if your aunt will sell me the cottage I'm living in at present, I'll buy it. What have you got to say to *that,* Miss Holly Templeton?'

CHAPTER FOUR

HOLLY felt as if the ground had been swept away from under her feet. Aghast, she stared at him, unable to say anything.

'I thought that might surprise you,' he said laconically. Then he moved aside. 'Off you go. I'll finish feeding the kittens.'

Holly nearly bumped into her aunt as she went through the living-room. 'My dear Holly,' she began. 'There's the most beautiful *enormous* Afghan hound outside in Sergeant MacLeish's van. He's starving – must have walked for miles, his pads are nearly worn away, poor darling. I'm just going to find him some food, and then we'll let him sleep.'

'I'll go and get some jeans on,' said Holly, hiding the shock she still felt at Gareth's announcement. She ran quickly upstairs. So he hoped to stay permanently, did he? She felt confused inside at the knowledge. It would be good for her aunt to have a man about the place. She was getting older, and life could be difficult for a woman alone, especially one nearing seventy – Gareth certainly seemed helpful, suspiciously so at times, thought Holly as she donned jeans and a warm red sweater. What normal man would do so much, willingly, for an old woman without expecting any kind of payment? And still nagging at her was the fact that he didn't work. There was so much that was odd about him, in a way she couldn't put her finger on. He didn't appear lazy. What odd jobs he had done had been well executed, and he worked quickly and without fuss, the sure sign of a craftsman. And yet – and yet – there was a deep mistrust of him within Holly. Something didn't add up. All that she'd seen and heard and knew about him gave a picture of a man of strength and character. Even though the dislike appeared to be mutual, Holly could not deny that. But to imagine him settling down and staying in a small house in the middle of a remote part of the bleak, rugged Highlands – that didn't fit. She was sorely tempted to mention it to her aunt, but something held her back. Holly knew it would be wrong of her to try and influence Aunt Margaret. If she wanted to sell to him, it was nothing to do with Holly.

Making a determined effort to put all the disturbing thoughts of an even more disturbing man to the back of her mind, she went down to see the new arrival.

An hour later she was wishing she hadn't been so hasty in having had her bath early. She was completely filthy from helping Gareth to erect a dog-proof fence at the side of the barn. It was something, Aunt Margaret admitted, that should have been done long ago, but she had kept putting it off. Now, the Afghan decided her – and also Holly and Gareth, who, in another temporary kind of truce, had taken one look at the enormous long-haired dog and nodded their agreement.

The police sergeant and his son had departed with very relieved looks on their faces, and full of promises to find the owner; the wire netting bought prudently by Aunt Margaret several years ago at a ridiculously cheap price had been unrolled from its resting place in a corner of the barn, and now, with some extremely hard work from Gareth, and assistance from the two women, it stretched along the section of field at the side of the barn, well secured to posts. It made a large rectangle that would take all the dogs in comfort, and enable them to exercise without being able to stray.

The Afghan had demonstrated his personality by accidentally knocking over – with no apparent effort, or appearance of wilfulness – Gareth's carefully stacked fence posts. Holly, unable to resist the laughter that threatened, had said gaspingly to her aunt: 'Is he terribly clumsy, or is it my imagination?'

'No, dear, it's not your imagination,' Aunt Margaret sighed. 'The poor creature can't help it. Gordon MacLeish said he was nearly run over by a tractor before he could rescue the animal – a tractor, I ask you!'

Holly sighed. 'Poor lamb. He's so big – but there's something very lovable about him all the same. What are you going to call him?'

'I once had an uncle like him – you wouldn't remember him, he died when I was quite small – but everywhere he went he created chaos, and he couldn't help it either.'

'What was his name?' Holly was intrigued.

'Herbert.'

'Then Herbert should do nicely. What do you think, Aunt?'

And so the Afghan became Herbert. Holly watched Gareth finish the last stretch of fence, and she wiped her forehead as her aunt bustled off back to the house to make the inevitable cup of tea.

Gareth gave his handiwork an experimental push to test it, then came over to Holly. 'All done,' he said. 'I'm going to have a bath. I'm afraid you look as if you could do with another one.'

'Thanks,' she retorted dryly. 'I was aware of that.'

'Oh, by the way, thank you for your help.' She

looked quickly at him, trying to detect sarcasm, but could see none.

'I did it for the dogs,' she said.

'Yes, I'm sure you did. Nevertheless, it would have taken me twice as long without you. So thank you.' And with that he turned away and walked off to his house. Holly stood and watched him go, and something stirred inside her. Why did he have this power to alternately infuriate her and make her feel small? More, why did she let him? She found herself waiting for his barbed remarks, instead of trying to ignore them, which should have been easier. Just now there had been nothing – and yet something. It was difficult for her to put a finger on it, but it was as if the tangible tension affected him too, making everything he said have a double meaning. His eyes rarely gave anything away. Dark, infinitely mysterious, they had hidden depths, an inner fire that smouldered and made him potentially dangerous. But could it all be due to her imagination? Holly walked slowly back to the house, pondering the questions in her mind, and she was a turmoil of mixed emotions. In just over an hour they would be leaving to go for dinner at the Colonel's. And perhaps then she would see yet another facet of Gareth's puzzling character.

Aunt Margaret had excelled herself. All her life she had worn bright colours, not necessarily matching, and her clothes were as much a part of her charm as anything else in her personality. For strangers, however, a first meeting was often something of a surprise. Now, as Holly went down, wearing a simple blue dress in heavy dacron, she exclaimed: 'Aunt Margaret, you look like a queen!'

And indeed she did. From somewhere in her vast wardrobe she had unearthed a deep rich velvet dress, blue-black, with long sleeves and floor-sweeping skirt. Around her neck glittered a diamanté collar – and on her it could well have been diamonds. She smirked appreciatively, and gave Holly a deep curtsey. 'You think the Colonel might be impressed?' she chuckled, highly amused.

'I do indeed.' Holly went over to her. 'You'll show 'em!'

Her aunt's frizzy grey hair had been skilfully controlled and swept upwards by little Mrs. Macrae. Faintly blue-tinted now, it set off her plump pleasant face, and lent her an air of gracious dignity.

'You look absolutely super!' Holly breathed. 'Just wait until Gareth sees you.' And we see him, she added inwardly. What would he look like? She hadn't long to wait. It was nearly a quarter to seven, and a few moments later there came a knock at the door, which was partially open, and Gareth walked in. He stood quite still by the door as they turned to look at him.

Holly was stunned. She had not expected this. Even as she heard him telling Aunt Margaret how wonderful she looked, she watched him. Gone were the old sweater and jeans. He was dressed, very simply, in a lightweight charcoal suit, white shirt, and dark grey tie. Nothing spectacular, but he looked stunningly handsome. Holly caught a glimpse of gold at his cuffs as he came forward slowly. The dazzling white of the shirt made him seem darker by comparison, and his black hair was brushed neatly – the first time she had seen it so. He moved with an easy grace, and it was at that moment, as his cool dark gaze rested on her, that Holly realized that this was no ordinary man. Subtly, he had changed – not only in his dress, but in his whole appearance. And he knew. She caught the swift gleam of mockery in those eyes before he turned away, and she bit her lip. To her aunt he said:

'I've checked that the dogs are all safe. Shall we go?'

'My dear Gareth! You look very smart!' Aunt Margaret exclaimed belatedly, clearly as stunned as Holly had been.

He bowed slightly. 'Thank you, ma'am.' A swift smile lit his dark features. 'I couldn't let you down, could I?' He glanced at his watch. 'Nearly ten to. Shall we take your car? I think it's a little more respectable – and comfortable – than the Land-Rover.'

'Just as you like.' Aunt Margaret made a last check in the living-room and kitchen, counted the kittens, told Kazan and Smokey to behave themselves, and they all went outside. 'We mustn't be back too late,' she told Gareth as she picked her careful way across the cobbled yard, her skirt held an elegant few inches from the ground. 'You think eleven? They won't be offended, will they?'

He held open the passenger door for her. 'I don't think you could offend anyone, dressed like that,' he answered smoothly, as he helped her in. He barely looked at Holly as he closed the door after them both, then eased his long legs into the driver's side. And they were off. A slight flutter of excitement began within Holly, and she wondered what the evening held in store.

The door was opened by Mike, who bounded down the steps to open their doors as they stopped.

'Evening, Miss Templeton. Hello, Holly, Gareth,' he greeted them. He looked momentarily stunned at Aunt Margaret's regal appearance, and Holly hid a smile as they went up the steps and into a wide oak-panelled hall with its log fire throwing out a welcome crackle of heat.

'Father thought it might be chilly,' he explained. 'Will you come into the drawing-room for drinks? Down, boy,' he added sternly as a large Dalmatian bounded up intent on greeting everyone.

He led them into an elegant high-ceilinged room, the size of the entire ground floor at the cottage, and indicated chairs. 'Do please sit down. Dad won't be a moment. Now, Miss Templeton, what will you have?'

Holly looked round as he busied himself with the drinks, her eye caught Gareth's, and he seemed faintly amused by something as he wandered over to a large bookcase that filled the wall by the fireplace. She was puzzled, then forgot why as she heard Mike asking her what she wanted to drink.

'Oh, a dry sherry, please.'

'And you, Gareth?' Mike was being the good host, determinedly so, it seemed to Holly.

'I'll have the same, thanks.' He bent down and lifted a book from the shelf, glanced idly at it, then replaced it and sat down. Holly wanted, suddenly, to know what it was. Ridiculous, of course – she knew it wasn't important – but what was his taste in books? Did he always read heavy tomes? She had looked at the book he had been reading at her aunt's the other night when he had been waiting up for her. It had been an obscure book of stories by Chekhov.

The next moment the door opened, and a man and

woman came in. Gareth stood up, Mike turned towards them, and Holly looked. So this was Colonel Radford. But who, she wondered, was the gorgeous woman by his side? He was a widower, Mike had told her, and he hadn't mentioned a stepmother, so who was it? The Colonel was tall, as tall as Gareth, well built and youthful-looking despite iron grey hair smoothed back over his ruddy-complexioned handsome face. Dressed immaculately in evening suit, he came over to Aunt Margaret, who raised a gracious beringed hand as Mike performed the introductions. They all shook hands, then the Colonel said 'This is a great pleasure. And may I introduce my niece, Laura, who has come to stay for a few days.'

Laura, in an elegant black dress that showed her slim shapely figure to perfection, came forward with a dazzling smile. Gareth was the last one she shook hands with, and her glance lingered on him, the smile now provocative as she murmured: 'How do you do, Gareth?'

Holly watched them, sherry glass held tightly in hand. Laura was dark, probably in her middle twenties – though it was difficult to tell – her hair short and straight at the back, longer at the front so that the ends curled gently under her chin. Her eyes were large and brilliantly blue, exquisitely made up to appear luminous. She had barely glanced at Holly or her aunt. Those eyes were only for Gareth.

The Colonel sat beside Aunt Margaret on the settee, and began talking to her, his whole manner that of a man determined to make amends for his behaviour. He too, in his way, was charming, but somehow Holly found herself watching Gareth and Laura, who had both remained standing. Then Mike was beside her, his duties as drink dispenser finished. He sat on the arm of Holly's chair and whispered: 'Everything okay, Holly?'

She smiled at him. 'Fine, thanks.' She glanced across at the couple now engrossed in conversation, Laura holding her glass of dry Martini in an utterly feminine, almost helpless manner, as if it were too heavy. Holly whispered: 'Your cousin is beautiful, isn't she?'

'Yes, gorgeous. Dad wanted her to meet Gareth,' he answered, almost in Holly's ear. 'They make a nice pair, don't they?' he added, in a strange tone.

'Yes, they do,' and suddenly she didn't want to talk about them any more. She sipped her sherry, determined to enjoy herself. Why, though, did she dislike Laura so? She had only just met her.

The room filled with the fragrance of cigars as the three men smoked and drank their drinks. The Colonel come over and spoke to Holly and Mike, and seemed so charming, not a bit as she had imagined, and Holly laughed and smiled in all the right places, and tried to give the impression that she was having a wonderful time.

Mike was attentive and considerate, and when they all went into dinner, she was between him and Gareth at the round table set with gleaming silver on heavy cream damask. A bowl of roses was on the centre of the table.

Laura was at Gareth's other side, and apart from the normal courtesies of salt-passing, Holly might not have been there, as far as he was concerned. He was totally immersed with Laura, his elegant, good-looking dark face turned constantly to her as they spoke and laughed together.

The meal was wonderful, or would have been if

Holly hadn't had a faintly sick feeling inside her all through it. She didn't know what had caused it; she had been fine when they set out. She tried hard to hide it, and succeeded, for Mike noticed nothing.

After the meal was over, they went back into the richly furnished, warm drawing-room, its heavy red velvet curtains open, showing the shadowed garden with its many trees outlined against a starry sky. Holly went over to look out of the huge curved window, and when a faint movement came beside her, said: 'I'd love to see round the gardens some time.'

There was a slightly shocked cough, then Gareth's amused voice: 'Not with *me*, surely!'

Holly turned swiftly, dismay on her face. 'I thought it was Mike!'

'Obviously,' he agreed dryly. 'He's gone to fetch some more booze from the cellar.'

'Really? And where's Laura?' Holly asked sweetly, composure regained.

He lifted one eyebrow in that infuriating way. 'I never ask a lady where she's going, for fear of embarrassing her.'

'You surprise me,' Holly said shortly, turning away to stare determinedly out of the darkened window. But now, strangely, all she could see were their reflections in the glass, and Gareth's mocking face beside her.

She swallowed hard, very conscious of his nearness, of his sleeve brushing against her bare arm, and she moved slightly away to ease the intolerable tension that had sprung up in that small private space. She heard him laugh softly, then he whispered: 'Here's your boyfriend,' and his reflection vanished. Holly was left alone.

The evening passed, and when the clock neared

eleven her aunt said reluctantly: 'This really has been the most delightful evening, Colonel Radford, but I'm afraid I'm not as young as I was—'

'My dear lady! Not thinkin' of going? I won't hear of it.'

He stood and took her glass from her. 'The night is young. You'll have another Advocaat?'

'Well, just a teeny one. Then I really think—' she smiled and winked at Holly as their host's back was turned, and Holly gulped hastily, nearly swallowing her drink the wrong way. The Colonel was clearly enchanted with Aunt Margaret, all differences forgotten as he fussed around her. A man of power and great charm, when he chose – and clearly determined to throw Laura and Gareth together as much as possible. But why? Holly was no nearer an answer to anything about the complex man, Gareth, who was her neighbour, than she had been before. The Colonel's manner, when he addressed him, was friendly – and more. Almost respectful. It didn't make sense. Nothing did any more. And Holly realized, as she gazed into the mellow gold liquid in her glass, that she was more than a little tipsy. She suppressed a threatening hiccup, and looked around for Mike, who was refilling his own glass. As she did so, she saw that Gareth was watching her. He had paused to light a cigar, and Laura was bending to rub an imaginary spot from her immaculate shoes, and their eyes met. It was as if, suddenly, there was no one else in the room. Confused, Holly looked quickly away, but that moment was impressed on her brain. There had been an unspoken message in Gareth's eyes in that split second of time. Holly's face felt warm, and it was a relief when Mike draped himself beside her and said: 'Your aunt wants to go, but you'll stay a while longer, won't you? I'll run you home.'

She smiled up at him, liking him, seeing his open friendly face looking down at her, in such contrast to . . . No, stop it, she told herself.

'Thanks, Mike, I'd love to, but—' she shrugged gracefully, 'I'd better go with her and help her walk the do—' she faltered, '—er – take the dog out.'

Mick chuckled. 'I've told you, I wouldn't let the old man know if she had a zoo – besides, have you *seen* him? He's quite bowled over by her.'

Holly looked at them. It was true. Colonel Radford was laughing at one of her aunt's remarks, throwing his head back, his face delighted. 'You do me good, Miss Templeton! Another drop? No?' This as she firmly shook her head, and gave him her sweetest smile.

Ten minutes later, with good-byes said, thanks given, much hand shaking, and invitations to come again flowing thick and fast, they settled themselves in the Mini, and Gareth flicked the lights in farewell as they set off down the moonlit drive.

'Oh dear – ah, that's better!' Aunt Margaret sank down on the settee and inelegantly kicked off her shoes. She looked round at Gareth who waited by the door, almost as if he intended leaving any moment. 'Come in, come in,' she called. 'Holly will make us all coffee, won't you, dear?'

Holly nodded, then wished she hadn't as the room swayed alarmingly. She wasn't used to drink, should never have mixed them, but somehow she had needed to try . . .

'I'll help you.' He was leaving the door, coming towards her, and she turned and went unsteadily to the kitchen. She bent to lift the coffee tin from the cupboard, obscurely angry with herself – and him.

A soft voice beside her said: 'Why don't you leave it all to me before you fall over?'

She whirled round on him, eyes sparkling, and banged the tin down on the working top beside her. 'Why don't you mind your own business?' she hissed softly, well aware that her aunt was only in the next room, although gentle snores seemed to be issuing from that direction . . .

'She's asleep.' His voice was low, amused. 'So you don't need to whisper. Had a drop too much to drink, as well as you, I should imagine.'

'Nobody asked your opinion,' Holly retorted, watching as he pushed the door shut with a soft click behind him. She filled the kettle at the tap and slammed it down on the gas stove. Why didn't he move, or go away, or something? Instead of standing *watching* her with that dark gaze? 'Damn the thing!' she muttered as the gas-lighter clicked and refused to light, and his hand closed over hers in a most disconcerting way, and she found it being gently removed from her grasp. 'I'll do that. You get out three cups, okay?' And for a moment his hand was on her bare arm, and her heart played tricks. She jerked herself away from him, and took three beakers from the draining board. Her head ached, and there was a dry lump in her throat that refused to go away when she swallowed. Mechanically she spooned coffee into the three mugs, and her hand had a slight tremor so that some was spilt. Nothing escaped his eagle eye, she thought bitterly, as he smiled.

'Better wipe it up before it goes all sticky,' he suggested.

'Oh, go to hell!' she muttered, and heard him

laugh.

'Mmm! If this is what sherry and brandy do for you, I must remember never to buy you any.'

She looked at him then. '*You* buy me drinks? I shouldn't worry – the occasion is hardly likely to arise.'

'No?' He lifted a cynical eyebrow. 'Don't be too sure.'

'What do you mean?' she demanded, but he shook his head, still amused.

'Forget it.' He turned away as the kettle began to whistle, and switched off the gas. 'Right, coffee coming up. You'd better wake your aunt gently. Go on – I'll make this.'

Surprised at her own meek acquiescence, Holly obeyed. She put it down to her slightly – not unpleasantly – fuddled state, but deep down inside her she knew there was another reason. Just for the moment, though, she hadn't the faintest idea what it was . . .

After they had drunk the coffee, Gareth looked at Aunt Margaret and smiled. Funny, thought Holly, he smiles quite differently at her.

'I'll take the dogs out, Miss Templeton. Shall I take the Afghan as well, or leave him?'

'Oh, Herbert? Oh dear, I don't know. He seemed exhausted. What do you suggest, Gareth? We don't want him running off – especially as he's just found shelter, do we?'

'I'll put a rope on his collar – there's one in the barn. A short walk won't do him any harm, I'm sure. If you'll excuse me, I'll go and change. This is my only suit.' And he went out quietly, shutting the door after him.

'Isn't he *marvellous*?' sighed Aunt Margaret. She looked shrewdly at Holly, her hair slightly untidy after her brief nap. 'Or do you still dislike him?'

Holly tried to smile, but with difficulty. For suddenly she knew what had puzzled her in the kitchen, why her heart had beat faster at Gareth's casual, almost accidental touch. Absurd, of course – it was most likely the drink that was causing this distinct fluttering inside her at the very mention of his name. But . . .

'No,' she said slowly, 'he's not as bad as I thought. I must admit he looked very different tonight at the Colonel's—'

'And he was obviously very taken with that niece, Laura. Well, she certainly is a beautiful girl.'

'Yes, she is,' agreed Holly, and kept her face expressionless. Because she knew that if she let anything show, her aunt would know – and she didn't want anyone to guess the emotion she felt – not until she had had a chance to think about it. Was it possible, she thought, wonderingly, that she was actually beginning to find Gareth attractive?

Holly didn't see anything of Gareth the next day. In the early evening the phone rang, and it was Mike to see if she wanted to go out for a ride with him. On the point of refusing, Holly thought better of it, and accepted. He told her he would be round half an hour later, and they said good-bye. It was better to go out than sit at home wondering if Gareth was going to come round. Holly bit her lip as she left the phone, unhappily wondering why she should feel like this. It was ridiculous. Less than two weeks ago she had loathed him, and now . . . She shivered and went to tell her aunt, a bright smile on her face. 'It was Mike,' she said. 'Is it all right if I go out for a ride with him?'

'Of course – you know it is, child! He seems a nice young man. Hurry up and powder your nose. When's he coming?'

'Half an hour,' Holly called, running up the stairs. In her bedroom as she pulled on a warm blue figure-hugging sweater in fluffy mohair, over tight black trews, she heard a car door slam and went to the window, wondering if Mike had come early – and saw Gareth's Land-Rover making its ponderous way down the path. So he was going out too. Her mouth felt suddenly dry. He had never been out in the Land-Rover at night before – and surely Laura was used to more elegant forms of transport? She turned away from the window quickly, afraid that he would see her. There was no doubt in her mind who he was going to see.

When Mike arrived half an hour later, promptly as usual, she greeted him with a happy smile. 'Hello, Mike,' she said as she ushered him into the living-room. 'Just got to get my coat.' And she left him talking to her aunt and ran upstairs. Inside her was a determination to enjoy the evening.

Bowling along deserted Highland roads, with the moon high over the black mountains lending its unearthly radiance to everything, Holly began to feel almost happy. Everything would be all right, she thought. Mike was kind, a nice person, and good fun to be with, and they would have a pleasant evening, perhaps even stop for a drink – 'Mike, where are we going?' she asked suddenly, sensing the purpose in his driving.

'The club. You remember – last week?' he looked at her laughingly.

'But is it open on a Sunday?' she asked, bewildered.

'Well, you know, not officially – but they get round it very nicely by insisting we have a meal. That makes us "travellers".'

'Oh dear!' she groaned. 'You should have told me before!'

He laughed. 'Don't worry. You can manage a chicken sandwich or an omelette, I'm sure.'

'I suppose so.' Then, very casually: 'Laura's very attractive, isn't she? Er – is she stopping long?'

He slanted her a brief sideways glance. 'I don't know. She *said* only a few days, but – well—' a casual shrug, '—she might make it longer. She's taken quite a shine to your next-door neighbour.'

'I gathered that much.' Holly said it lightly, but inwardly felt very different. She was saved from asking the next question by Mike's words. 'He's taken her out tonight. Of course, most men fancy Laura, can't say I blame him.'

A cold numbness spread across her chest. 'And you,' she said, oh, so very casually, 'don't you fancy her?'

He laughed, a short almost bitter sound. 'My dear coz is four years older than me – and I'm not sophisticated enough for her.' And there was something in the way he said it that give Holly a sudden insight. Mike, for all his casualness, his effort at lightness, was not immune from the beautiful Laura's charms himself. Oh, poor Mike! Somehow it gave Holly the slight impetus needed to shake off her minor depression, and when they arrived at the old mansion she took his arm as they went up the steps. The lights were subdued, as if in deference to the Highland Sabbath, and perhaps the law, although Sergeant MacLeish was no doubt curled up by his fire, quite disinterested in illegal drinking, and as he was the only representative of the law for many miles, there was little fear of a 'raid'.

There were fewer people inside, but the clatter of cutlery came from the dining-room, and Holly glanced idly in as they passed on their way to the cocktail lounge. Involuntarily her footsteps faltered as she saw the couple eating in a quiet corner – and the man looked up, and their eyes met silently for a moment, than he smiled – and Holly turned away before her face flamed. For Gareth's smile hadn't been pleasant merely a slight quirk of the mouth, as if to say – 'What, you again!'

Sitting at the bar with Mike, Holly said tightly: 'Fancy seeing them here!'

'Fancy,' he agreed dryly. 'Considering there's not much doing on a Sunday hereabouts, I suppose I should have known we would. Do you – do you mind?'

'Mind?' She gave a little laugh. 'Heavens, no!' But the thought lingered; had Mike known? Had he asked her out for reasons of his own – to do with Laura? She hid a wry smile as she fumbled in her bag for a handkerchief. Some women had it very easy, she thought. Laura just had to flutter those brilliant eyes with their super long lashes, and the men were bowled over. She didn't realize, couldn't know, as she sat at the bar sipping a tomato juice, that she herself had more than one man's eyes on her. Sitting there on a high stool, her curves emphasized by the blue fluffy sweater, her face smooth-skinned and glowing with health, Holly was a picture of rare feminine beauty – and she needed no make-up to emphasize the clear serenity of her dark eyes. Quite unaware of her own powers of attraction, she smiled and talked to Mike – and wished wretchedly that she was at home with her aunt.

By coincidence – or design, she didn't know – by the time Gareth and Laura had finished their meal, she and Mike were on their way into the dining-room. The four exchanged brief greetings, and Laura smiled at Holly, and touched Gareth's arm possessively, and her lashes came down, narrowing her eyes. The message was unspoken but quite explicit: He's with me. And neither of the men knew, that was certain.

Then Laura looked slowly down at Holly's trews, and travelled slowly with her eyes up, up to Holly's face. 'You do look *sweet*, Holly,' she said. 'Doesn't she, Gareth?'

He nodded, but, Holly noted, his eyes were only for Laura. 'Yes, indeed.' The dark glance flashed briefly over her, then to Mike. 'We're going for a drink in the bar now. We might see you later?' He nodded, and they both turned away, secretive, *together*.

Sitting down in the dining-room, Holly seethed with suppressed anger. Who did he think he was? Who did they both think they were? They certainly deserved each other, she thought bitterly. Laura's patronizing amusement was hard to take – but *him* – *him* – to dismiss them both, like children . . .

'Something light, Holly?'

'What?' She realized that a waiter was hovering impatiently as Mike touched her arm. 'Oh, I'm not really hungry – may I have just an omelette?' She waited until the bored looking waiter had gone, then looked at Mike. It was incredible, but he didn't seem to have noticed anything wrong. He was studying the menu thoughtfully, as if inwardly debating whether he had ordered the right thing. Holly's glance softened, and she began to relax. He was the sensible one, not her. Inwardly though, she determined to spin the omelette out as long as possible. She had no wish to spend longer with *them* than necessary.

When eventually they made their way to the cocktail bar, Gareth and Laura had gone. Holly banished the slight instinctive pang firmly. Good, she thought, that suits me. But all the same, she wondered where . . .

They spent another half hour in the bar, chatting to another couple, then left. Outside the air had turned bright and cold, and their footsteps crunched grittily on the gravel. Holly drew her coat tighter round her and shivered as Mike slid in and opened her door for her.

They had only gone three or four miles when the engine of the Jaguar gave a slight apologetic cough, and the car glided gently to a halt.

'What the hell—' began Mike, twiddling the ignition angrily. Then he stopped and groaned. 'Oh, no!'

'What is it, Mike?' Holly looked anxiously at him as he hung his head, then pulled a rueful face. 'Sorry, Holly – I hardly dare tell you, but we've run out of petrol!' At her disbelieving gasp, he went on: 'Yes, I know it's a corny old line, but it's true. I meant to get filled up at Kishard today, but forgot that everything goes dead on Sunday here. Oh, lord! Look, tell you what. I'll go back to the club and see if anyone will sell me some. I keep a tin in the boot, but it's empty now – of course. Will you wait here, or come with me?'

Holly jumped out. 'I'd rather walk than wait. Come on,' she began to laugh. 'Oh, Mike, you should see your face!'

'You're not mad?' He looked at her astonished, and she shook her head.

'No, it can happen to anyone up here – and anyway, a walk will do us good.'

He opened the boot and lifted out the petrol tin, then took her hand. As they began walking, he said: 'You know, Holly, you're a surprising girl. I thought you'd be good and mad just then.'

She laughed. 'Of course I'm not.' There's only one man with the power to infuriate me, she thought, and it sobered her somewhat. More quietly she added: 'It's the sort of thing I'd always be doing – running out of petrol, I mean—' but before she could finish, the headlights from a vehicle blinded them, and they both moved to the side of the road as it came towards them. Mike lifted his arm – and the vehicle slowed down and stopped. Holly recognized Gareth's Land-Rover even before he swung out of the driver's seat. 'What's up?' He came towards them, and Holly saw the white blur of Laura's face behind the windscreen before she looked away.

'Ran out of juice. Am I glad to see you!' Mike grinned. 'We were just walking back to the club for petrol.' He rattled the empty tin hopefully.

'Sorry,' answered Gareth. 'I've no spare – and nothing to siphon any off with, but I'm low myself anyway. Let's push the Jag into a passing place first, we can collect it in the morning. Then hop in.' He gave Holly a brief glance. 'There are only two seats, but I dare say you and Laura could squeeze up together in the front. You're both pretty slim.'

'Thanks, but I'll manage in the back', Holly answered. It was a more civilized answer than, 'Over my dead body', however strong the temptation.

Five minutes later they were bowling along in the Land-Rover, and Holly sat on Mike's knee on the floor, with his arms tightly round her in the back of the vehicle. Gareth's voice came faintly over the noise of the engine: 'Sorry if it's a bit bumpy at the back – I'm going as slow as I can.'

'Don't worry,' shouted Mike in reply. 'We're doing all right,' and he squeezed Holly tightly and grinned at her, and tried to kiss her ear. On and on they went, and eventually Holly saw Rhu-na-Bidh in the distance, hidden by trees, now visible, now hidden again, and as they neared it, she expected Gareth to turn up the track – but he went straight on. She felt Mike stiffen in surprise, then he said:

'You can drop us off, Gareth, I'll walk home from—'

'Wouldn't dream of it,' floated back the reply. 'It's only a few minutes now.' Holly caught a glimpse of Laura's provocative profile as she turned to Gareth. She too was startled – and oddly, Holly had a small stab of satisfaction. Probably Mike would feel the sharp edge of her tongue for ruining the end of her evening – and in fact, the thought came suddenly, why hadn't Gareth stopped? Unpredictable in everything he had done it again. And – Holly's heart skipped erratically – this now meant that she would be going home alone with him, if even only for a short journey. She bit her lip in the dark confines of the back. Strange how things sometimes worked out, she mused.

As they drove up towards Mike's home, Laura leaned across and whispered something to Gareth, who laughed, then answered her, keeping his voice low. The muscles tightened in Holly's throat, and she felt choked. The air of casual intimacy between them was oddly distressing. She glanced at Mike, who gave her a slight smile. So he had seen the little exchange as well!

Then Gareth was stopping by the brilliantly lit front entrance, and he jumped out and came round to Laura's side. Holly and Mike crept along and eased themselves thankfully out, to stand by the Land-Rover in the pool of light cast from the house. For a moment it seemed as if no one would speak, then Mike said: 'Well, Holly, you might as well get in the front. Travel the last couple of miles in style anyway.' He took her arm and guided her a few feet away from the other two. 'Sorry about the car. I could kick myself, honestly.'

'Don't, Mike. It doesn't matter,' and her eyes were on Gareth as Laura reached up to brush something from his shoulder. 'We'd better go. It's getting cold.' But it wasn't the frost that was making her shiver.

She waved good-bye to the two people standing on the steps to the front door, Mike tall and rugged, Laura beside him, slim and feminine, eyes only for Gareth. Holly suddenly thought, she's good and mad, I can tell – but she's too clever to show it. And she choked back a laugh that was half a sob, and Gareth said: 'What is it?'

'Nothing.' She sat up straighter and took a deep breath. She wondered if he was annoyed too, at having the end of his evening spoilt – then remembered that both had left the club well before her and Mike. They'd had plenty of time to . . . She resolutely turned to look out of the window to see the trees flashing past, and the rhododendrons, huge grey clumps in the night. She would not, she positively would not let her mind dwell on what might have happened. Has Gareth kissed her like he kissed me that night? No, stop it, *stop it*, she told herself, and her fists clenched tightly to prevent herself from gasping out loud.

They came out of the drive, and sped along the road – and suddenly Gareth was pulling to the side, into a large passing place. She turned to him in astonishment. 'What—?' she began.

'I want to know what's the matter,' he said bluntly. 'And I can't find out when I'm driving, and we'll be home in a minute – so we'll stop here. Are you annoyed because I didn't drop you and Mike off near the cottage?'

Holly was silent. If only he knew, she thought. If only he knew!

'Not at all,' she answered coolly. 'If that's all you stopped for, hadn't we better go?'

He shrugged. 'Not yet.' Then, as if needing to say something – anything, he added: 'It's a lovely night. Look at those trees, and that moon – beautiful!' Holly had to agree, inwardly at least. She had felt it when she'd started the walk back to the club with Mike, the magic of the Highland night, cold and clear as crystal – but then had been much different from *now*. Now, she was with a man she couldn't fathom, and it subtly altered the quality of everything. In the distance she could see bleak towering mountains, and not far away was the loch, black and calm, as it always was at night. And suddenly, for the first time ever, Holly turned to look at Gareth without any idea of what she was going to say, without the protective armour she had come to wear whenever he was near. 'Yes,' she said. 'It is beautiful – it's so beautiful that it always makes me want to cry.'

There was a pause, a quiet moment before Gareth said softly: 'Yes, I know what you mean. I'm glad you feel that way too. Holly – why are we always fighting?' And as he said it, he put out his hand and touched her cheek very gently. 'I don't want to fight you.'

'I don't – know.' His hand was warm as it rested on her cheek, and she reached up and covered it with her own. 'I don't know,' she repeated, and her heart was bursting.

Gareth's face was near now, dark and shadowed, for the only light came from the high thin moon, filtered by cloud, but she knew every inch of that face, knew the gipsy darkness, the thick brows, those deep eyes that had the power to make her heart turn somersaults – and his lips. She saw them move, heard the very soft, almost whispered words: 'Holly, I—' and then he stopped, and in the close confines of the Land-Rover she felt his hard muscular arm slide along her shoulders, pulling her towards him. It was like nothing she had ever known or dreamed of before. Nothing else existed, not Laura nor Mike nor anybody. There were just the two of them in the world, and the kiss went on and on, until at last, shakily, he pulled himself away, and in a voice that shook, said: 'My God, but I've been wanting to do that for a while.' His eyes devoured her as he said huskily: 'I'm not dreaming, am I? You really are here?'

'Yes,' she whispered. She could scarcely breathe. How had it all happened? She didn't know, only that it had, and it was so wonderful that it hurt. Carefully, almost as if afraid to disturb the spell, he moved, and Holly moved, and this time the kiss seemed to last for ever.

When at last it was over, he could hardly speak. There was silence for several explosive moments, and she heard his quickened breathing, sensed that for him, the kiss had started something that would be difficult to stop. But she reached out to touch his face, not knowing why, driven by an instinct she barely understood, and he gripped her hand, and in a voice quite unlike his own, said: 'Don't – please don't. I – we must go now, Holly, I won't be—' and he stopped.

'Gareth, what is it?' she whispered.

He groaned. 'Don't you know?' He turned away and gripped the steering wheel with both hands. 'I must be mad. I'm sorry, Holly – I apologize, I shouldn't have touched you. I—' and he stopped, and she saw him close his eyes as if in pain. Then he spoke, more slowly, under control again as he turned to look at her. She saw his slight smile, heard him say the words: 'I don't know what you thought about me before – but I shudder to think what your opinion is now.'

Holly bit her lip. 'You didn't notice me struggling to get away from you, did you?' She still trembled.

His face was blurred in that grey light, the outline hazy and unclear. 'No. Do you – do you mean what I think you do?'

She laughed, softly. 'I think so. Oh yes, I think so.'

'Then in that case,' and even in the darkness, she caught his wry smile, 'we'd definitely better be going, before – before I make love to you.' He reached forward to switch on, and the engine rumbled into life. The sound was music to Holly's ears – everything was wonderful. They drove on towards home, and the magic was all around them. It sparked in the air like electricity, and her whole being tingled with the realization of what had happened. As they bumped up the last few yards of track towards the cottage, she said: 'Will you come in for a coffee?'

He grinned at her, put out his hand and squeezed hers. 'Are you twisting my arm?'

'Yes.'

'Then I have no choice.' He braked and switched off. 'Stay there.'

The next moment he was out, walking round, opening Holly's door, and putting his arms up to help her down. With his hands at her waist she jumped down on to the iron-hard ground. For just an instant he held her, and she felt his leashed muscular strength. Then they were walking towards the house, and he knocked and pushed open the door and ushered Holly in before him. She had the sensation of being in a dream – a very pleasant dream that would go on and on . . . and she nearly laughed at her aunt's astonished face.

Later, lying in bed, quite unable to sleep, Holly moved over on to her back and put her hands behind her head. Her eyes on the ceiling, she relived the evening from the moment Mike had first phoned, to the heart-stopping magic minutes in the Land-Rover. She closed her eyes, feeling again Gareth's arms round her, going over the wonderful, unbelievably new sensation of kissing and being kissed by the man she loved – she loved. It came as a shock of realization, and she moved her head restlessly. It couldn't be denied any longer. Softly, Holly whispered into the comforting darkness: 'I love Gareth.' And then satisfied because she had admitted it at last, she slept.

CHAPTER FIVE

MONDAY was washday, a chore which Holly had gladly undertaken, especially today, because everything was so wonderful. As she pegged the damp clothes out, a warm glow, that not even the crisp west wind could dispel, filled her, and she sang softly. She wondered when she would see Gareth. He had not stayed long the previous night, only long enough to drink his coffee, and talk for a few minutes, then he had left. She had gone with him to the door, and in the dark shelter of the porch he had touched her face for a moment with a gentle hand.

'Good night, Holly. Sleep well,' he had said, and gone. Her skin tingled at the contact, and she had watched him go, seen him wave just before vanishing into his house, a tall dark shadow.

Aunt Margaret had looked, and smiled, but said nothing. Holly went over to her to hug her and whisper: 'I was wrong about Gareth.' And the old woman had chuckled, but asked no questions.

Now as she struggled with a voluminous petticoat of her aunt's, that didn't want to be pegged out, Holly smiled to herself. Wise Aunt Margaret! She knew the value of silence.

'I'm going to the village,' her aunt's voice interrupted her thoughts. 'Anything you want, dear?'

'No, thanks,' Holly shook her head, and dropped several pegs. She stooped to pick them up as Aunt Margaret left to go back into the house. Then Kazan dashed up, in a moment of playfulness, and snatched a clean bra from the basket and made off with it in his mouth, looking back to see if Holly was going to play the game.

'Oh, you bad boy!' Half laughing, half annoyed, Holly launched herself after him, round the back of the house and part way across the yard until she saw Gareth pounce on him and wrest the bra from his mouth before aiming a playful swipe at the dog's rear end.

'Sorry,' he called. 'I'd gone to see how the Afghan was, and Kazan nipped out.' He walked slowly towards her, and she felt her heart lurch crazily. Their eyes met as he handed her the sadly soiled bra. He grinned. 'Looks like you'll have to wash it again.'

'Yes. Thanks.' She felt suddenly confused, and pushed back her hair in a nervous gesture. His eyes held a warmth she'd not seen before. Warmth – and something else that would have been puzzling if she hadn't been too happy to wonder at it.

'Look,' he began, 'I'll be going into Strathmhor later today for some things. Would you like to come, Holly?'

'Please,' she nodded, eyes shining, quite unconscious of the picture she made at that moment. Gareth was aware, only too aware. He smiled slightly and turned away as he said: 'Fine, I'll let you know when.' And Holly decided she had imagined the bleak expression that fleetingly touched his features.

She finished the clothes, shooed several kittens from the vegetable garden to which they had escaped, and put them in the wire cat run. She went in to tidy up the living-room, in its usual chaotic state after the weekend, and bundled up Aunt Margaret's knitting which had been left on the settee. Holly had never seen anything actually finished – but the animals in the barn benefited. Many were the multi-coloured blankets they lay on; blankets that were strangely shaped, and had clearly been intended for cardigans or jumpers. She smiled to herself as she opened the sideboard door to push the bundle of knitting in. Then the smile faded as a small snapshot fluttered to the floor from where it had been dislodged, and she bent to pick it up. All thoughts of knitting went from her mind as she gazed at the photograph of her father and mother, a happy holiday snap she had taken herself several years before, when she was ten, and had been given a camera. Settling back on her heels, oblivious to everything around her, Holly let the bittersweet memories rush forward into the front of her mind. They had all been happy then. James Templeton had a thriving fashion business in Manchester, making clothes which he supplied not only to large stores, but also to smaller shops round the country. Holly and her parents lived in a beautiful detached house on the outskirts of the city, and she had had a happy secure childhood. And then, somehow, things had begun to change, and life became very puzzling.

Perhaps, reflected Holly as she got slowly to her feet, still clutching the photograph with care as if it would crumble away to dust if she breathed on it, perhaps if they had told me what was happening, it would have been better. But instead they had tried to pretend nothing was wrong, and she became more puzzled and unhappy, as if her life, once so secure and safe, was shifting about on quicksand.

They had left the big house and moved to a smaller one. The housekeeper and gardener had 'retired' – and then suddenly her father closed his business, and started writing lots of letters. And Holly watched all this like a frightened child who fears what is happening, but dare not ask. It was only when she was fifteen, and her father was found dead in the garage of their home, with a shotgun by his side, that Holly had learned the truth. The verdict was 'accidental death', but Holly's mother told her the truth of what had led up to this dreadful moment – and Holly knew, they both did, that James Templeton had died because his spirit had been broken. The bitterness would not be held back. Holly's mother, her voice husky, her beautiful face ravaged by sorrow, had told her daughter of the ruin her husband had faced in his business, because of a new firm that had opened in Manchester, and deliberately set out to undercut his prices – and succeeded. She told her of the increasing struggle, mounting debts as James Templeton desperately tried to compete with the rivals, Neville Greene Associates, its boss, Neville Greene, a millionaire who had started from nothing about ten years previously.

'Remember that name,' her mother had said, tears filling her eyes and spilling out. 'Remember, he killed your father.'

Holly shivered, suddenly cold. Soberly she replaced the snapshot in the cupboard and went to the kitchen. She needed a cup of coffee to take away the taste of bitter memories. She had never forgotten the name. The man's companies stretched all over the country and abroad. He had a reputation for hard-hitting business methods that could even beat the Americans at their own game, and as such, was written of in reverent terms by financial papers. But to Holly he was the man who had ruined her father – and for no apparent reason save that *he* had decided to enter the 'rag trade', and James Templeton had been someone in the way.

She drank the coffee very hot, and busied herself with tidying and vacuuming. Her aunt returned soon afterwards, and then Gareth came to see if she wanted anything from Strathmhor. While he and Aunt Margaret talked, Holly ran upstairs to comb her hair and slip on a warm coat.

His eyes met hers as she came back into the room, slightly breathless from her hurry to be ready, her cheeks faintly pink. And he smiled. 'Ready?'

'Yes.' She bent to pick up her bag, and waved to Aunt Margaret. 'Good-bye, love.'

'Bye-bye, dear. Don't go too fast, Gareth – and you won't forget the dog food, will you? Only I start to stock up for winter now. You have enough money?'

He turned back as he was about to follow Holly out. 'I won't drive too fast, I won't forget, and yes, I have enough money.'

'Good,' Aunt Margaret nodded briskly. 'Off you go, then.'

He took Holly's arm as they crossed the yard. 'All right?' he said softly. He opened the doors and they got in.

Holly looked at him. He had taken a little more care with his appearance – not that it mattered, she thought. The gipsy look was still there, but toned down – unless, she suddenly realized, it only seemed to be, because she wasn't busy resenting him any more. She gave a shiver of pure joy, and he slanted a sideways glance at her as he controlled their journey down the road.

'Not cold?' he asked.

She laughed. 'No, it was just – a shiver, that's all.'

'Mmm,' he looked ahead. For a few moments he seemed to be hesitating, then he said: 'Look, I've got a bit of a problem.'

She glanced quickly at him, disturbed by something in his voice. 'What is it?'

'Well, I'm supposed to be seeing Laura on Thursday—' he stopped. Holly's breath caught in her throat.

'Y-es?' she faltered.

'And – and I don't know how to get out of it,' he said. Strange, she noticed his hesitation. How unlike him! Holly forced a carefree smile. 'No problem,' she said. 'Just go.' And she swallowed hard.

'Why don't you and Mike come too? We could make a foursome,' he said, and she was puzzled by that which was in his voice.

'Could we?' Her tone was light and casual. 'I'll see.' She held her bag tighter. She should have known that something would spoil it. But spoil what? There had been nothing said, nothing tangible, only a magic kiss in the dark, and the touch of this man's hand, and she had suddenly become aware of what life could hold. Sharply and intensely aware. And she knew too a deep primitive surge of jealousy that was as old as time – and she hated Laura. And soon – too soon – she would remember this conversation, and know the reason for Gareth's hesitation – but now, as they went on their way to Strathmhor she made a determined effort to put Laura to the back of her mind, and succeeded.

The next couple of hours were truly enjoyable as, with Gareth, she wandered round the shops and market of the large fishing village, greeting the friendly, shy people she remembered, seeing their hidden curiosity as they smiled, for they all knew Miss

Templeton's tenant by now. They had coffee and toasted tea-cakes at a lochside café with screeching gulls outside, and fishing boats bobbing on the water, and Gareth bought Holly a pendant as they were on their way out, for the proprietor, a canny Highlander, had a tray of trinkets by the door. Gareth slipped it round her neck, a deep rich blue-grey stone set in a silver circle on a heavy chain, and he said lightly: 'Think of me when you wear it.'

As they went out into the cold air, she touched it, and a strange feeling of contentment filled her. Holly didn't know then that this, these few precious hours, would be the last happy ones she would know for a long time. There was nothing to warn her.

When they set off home, the back of the Land-Rover was piled high with sacks of meal, and giant tins of dog food, and huge packets of dried meat for both cats and dogs. As they had loaded the vehicle, Holly lifted a petrol can and tried to shake it, but it was too heavy – too full.

'Gareth,' she asked curiously, 'I thought you didn't carry a spare, but this was in the back on Sunday – I nearly fell over it when I climbed in.'

'You did?' He clicked his fingers. 'Fancy me forgetting.' But the dark amused gaze told her more than words could, and she hastily turned away, her heart thudding against her ribs. She felt as if she couldn't breathe, couldn't cope with what was happening. It was too wonderful – too unbelievable to be true.

They drove back in companionable silence. There seemed no need for words. And when they were home, he carried everything into the cold pantry behind the kitchen, the small room where winter supplies were kept, ready for the almost inevitable snow, and he stepped back admiringly to take stock of the rows and rows of tinned food and milk, the sacks of flour, the jars of preserves, and he said: 'You're well organized, Miss Templeton, but is it *really* necessary?'

Holly and her aunt looked at one another. 'Young man,' said Aunt Margaret, 'if you'd spent last winter here you wouldn't *ask*. You'll not get far when there's six feet of snow plonk outside your front door, that's for sure.'

He held up his hands in a gesture of mock surrender. 'Point taken. I will now proceed to stock up myself. Any suggestions on what items are most important? I'd appreciate your advice.'

'We'll have a cup of tea and talk it over.' Aunt Margaret was in her element now, helping somebody.

They finished stacking the food, and then went into the living-room.

In the early evening, Aunt Margaret found that her supply of newspapers was very low, and more were needed for the kittens.

'I'll go and see if Gareth has any, shall I?' Holly offered.

'No dear, no need. The spare bedroom's chock full of old *Sunday Times.* I hate throwing them away – so full of interesting things I never seem to have time to read and mean to later—' her voice floated after Holly as she ran laughing up the stairs. Dear Aunt Margaret, she thought. She'll never change. She had been a hoarder all her life, and Holly knew that the spare bedroom would be bursting at the seams with just about everything else too. She went in and switched on the light in the sloping-ceilinged room which was always gloomy even in daytime, for the huge elm outside took all the light. Holly stood with arms akimbo for a few moments, wondering where to start to look . . .

Picking up a pile near the door, she took a last glance round to make sure no kittens had strayed in, then went down. It was later that it happened, when she read what she did, and it meant that life was never the same, ever again.

Aunt Margaret had gone to bed. Holly sat by a dying fire with Smokey and Kazan at her feet, fed and content. She was tired, and knew that she would soon have to go to bed herself, but for a few minutes she wanted to savour the day, while it was still fresh. She had by her side a cup of hot cocoa. Her aunt's empty cup was beside it, waiting to be rinsed with her own, and on the same table was a small pile of colour supplements from the pile of newspapers she had brought down. They were no good for the kittens, and Aunt Margaret had been going to put them out for the weekly bonfire, but Holly had said idly:

'I'll do that. I'll skim through them first and put them out in the morning.'

Now, sipping the hot sweet cocoa, she picked up the top magazine, two years old, and began leafing idly through it. The photograph leapt from the page at her, and at first she looked at it in disbelief, for what she saw was too bizarre to even begin to understand. She was seeing a picture of Gareth with an older man. Not the Gareth she usually saw, sweatered and bejeaned, but the other, different one she had seen the previous Saturday when they had gone to the Colonel's for dinner.

Here in this photograph too, he was dressed with superb elegance, as was the other man, older, his face very like Gareth's. The background was a luxuriously furnished room. Stunned, still slightly disbelieving, as if she were dreaming, Holly began to read the caption under the photo. 'Gareth Greene with his father Neville, millionaire boss of N.G.A.' But now the words were playing her tricks, surely? After all, it had only been today that she had found the snap, and . . . But it was real. This was no illusion. Holly clenched her teeth to stop herself from crying out. Then she put her hand to her mouth. The article was headed: 'What's it like for the sons of the Big Tycoons?' And there were other photographs on the next page too, of other young men and their fathers, but now there was only one that mattered as Holly searched feverishly down the page for the words that would tell her it was all a big mistake after all . . .

'. . . not so however for Gareth Francis Nicholas Greene, 30, only son of the boss of Neville Greene Associates, the multi-million dollar earner. He doesn't share his father's tastes in race horses or yachts. "It's the simple life for me," he admitted when he was interviewed. "You can keep the status symbols . . ." ' But she could read no more. The words blurred and danced as sick nausea threatened her, and with a little cry of pain she ran into the kitchen and bathed her burning face at the cold tap. Suddenly, very clearly in the midst of the appalling shock of it all, came a picture of the Colonel's face – and she knew now why Gareth had found it so easy to get round him.

'Of course,' she whispered. 'Of course! The Colonel recognized him, he must have done—' She walked blindly back into to the living-room, and there was the taste of ashes in her mouth as she remembered the way he had laughed, only hours before – how he had kissed her – Gareth had kissed her, Gareth Greene, only son of Neville, the man responsible for her father's death.

With shaking hands she picked up the magazine and forced herself to look at the man who stood beside Gareth. He would look like his father in thirty years, for the dark gipsy look was there in the older man, the hard ruthless glance that Gareth possessed – only more so in the father. Oh, yes, it was there all right, in them both, and Holly put her hand to her mouth and wiped viciously, instinctively to erase the memory of a traitor's kiss. How he must be amusing himself! To what purpose she couldn't even begin to guess – except that perhaps he gained pleasure, if not from yachting, from gloating over what was left of his father's victims.

Holly choked back a sob, crossed to the door and opened it. The night air struck her forcefully with its intense coldness, and at any other time she would have paused and gone for her coat, but the burning purpose in her consumed her with fire, and she felt nothing as she walked quickly, blindly across the yard to Gareth's house. In her hand she held the magazine.

She knocked at his door, and he shouted: 'Come in.' But she waited on the step, shivering now, and when after a few moments he flung the door open, he gave her a puzzled frown as he began: 'Hello, Holly, why didn't—'

'T-tell me, Gareth Nicholas *Greene*,' she said, in a voice that was only just steady. 'Tell me, how long were you going to go on amusing yourself with me?'

She saw his face change, saw shock followed by dismay, and the sick feeling came back renewed. Had she perhaps hoped he would deny it? Maybe, just for a moment – but his expression told her what no words could. He reached out to take her arm as he said urgently:

'Come in, Holly, I—'

'Don't touch me.' Her voice was low and controlled, because this for Holly was so important and terrible that she found reserves of strength from she knew not where to enable her to speak calmly. 'Don't *ever* touch me.' And then she looked at him, her eyes wide, tears brimming, yet not falling. 'I just want to know why. Just tell me w-why.' She lifted her head to force back the choking sobs that threatened, and her face was white. Slowly, with a trembling hand, she held out the magazine to him. 'Take it,' she whispered, 'and read it. I just did. I – don't want it any more.' And she turned away and walked back towards her aunt's house, stiff and numb with the effort not to break down.

But as she reached the door, she felt it being opened for her, then Gareth was coming in behind, nearly touching her. She felt her flesh creep at his nearness, and the prickle of dread at her neck.

'Let me explain – please.' He followed her in and shut the door, and she turned round on him.

'What is there to explain?' she asked. 'Are you Gareth Greene or not?'

'Yes, I am. But I want to tell you—'

'Tell me? Tell me what?' her voice rose slightly now at last. 'Tell me that you're sorry your father killed my father – or are you going to pretend you didn't know? I think—'

'Listen, Holly. For God's sake listen!' Gareth gripped her arms and there was nothing gentle in it. 'Say what you like after – but first let me explain—'

'Yes, do. Explain first why you changed your name – and why you told the Colonel to keep quiet about—' she winced as his grip tightened, and gasped, but went on: 'Oh, yes, I'm not a fool. No wonder he was all over you. Was that the p-price of his silence? That we went to dinner? Ah, you're hurting me!' She drew herself in instinctively as his fingers bit into her arms, and he swore softly, but loosened his grip.

'Listen,' he said. 'It's not like it seems. Yes, I admit it – Colonel Radford recognized me, he knows my father. What was I to do? All right, so I played along. It was only for a while, until I could tell you—' and he stopped, and looked at Holly, and she saw that look again, almost of pain in his eyes as he said: 'I wanted to tell you. I wanted to the other night – and then today, when – when we were going to Strathmhor, but—'

'Please don't,' she breathed. 'Please don't say any more. Just go away.' All the colour had drained from her face, and she felt physically so ill that it was a great effort to remain standing. But she would not, could not, show the slightest weakness before this man – this *enemy*.

He too was paler. It made his hair look darker than ever, and his eyes – his eyes, so eloquent, so *hateful*. She forced herself to meet them as she managed to get the final words out: 'Why don't you go away – leave here? We don't want you any more.' And she reached up and pulled sharply at the pendant she wore round her neck. The chain snapped and she dropped it to the carpet as if it burned her fingers. 'Take your pendant too,' she said. 'I don't want that either.' Blindly she turned and stumbled up the stairs, and she didn't look back at all.

'My goodness, Holly, what is it, child?' Aunt Margaret took one look at Holly's face the next morning, and put the teapot down with a bang and walked quickly towards her, where she stood in the living-room. It was nearly ten o'clock, and Holly had just woken from the worst night's sleep she had ever had, nightmare-filled, draining her of what little energy there was left after her discovery the previous night.

'Oh, Aunt Margaret!' Holly put her arms round the plump, comforting body, and the tears she had managed to hold back for so long came flooding out, and with them, a kind of release.

'Tell me,' her aunt said softly, and drew her niece beside her on the settee, sensibly giving her several minutes of uninterrupted weeping first. Holly took a deep breath, and began. She told her aunt everything about what she had seen in the paper, and of the confrontation with Gareth.

'And he n-never denied it,' she finished, her voice slightly calmer with the telling.

'Oh, my child, my dear child! What can I say?' The motherly old woman gazed into the distance with unseeing eyes, as if she too was being reminded of things that were too painful for words.

Then she looked at Holly's bowed head, and reached out a hand to touch the soft rich hair framing her niece's pale features.

'Perhaps,' she said tentatively, 'he spoke the truth, and he did intend to tell you. You should have let him—'

Holly turned astonished eyes to her aunt. 'Don't you *see*?' she exclaimed. 'What do words count for against the facts? He *is* Gareth Greene – h-his father deliberately set out to ruin Daddy – what does anything matter against that?' She put out her hands and clasped her aunt's. 'Just send him away,' she begged. 'I hate him more than words can tell.'

Aunt Margaret shook her head. 'I must see him,' she replied. 'I'll go now – after I've given you a cup of tea.

It won't take a minute.' But as she stood up, there was a knock at the door, and she called out: 'Come in.'

Holly knew it would be Gareth even before he spoke. She stood quietly, keeping her face averted from him, and said: 'I'll be in my bedroom, Aunt.' There was no power on earth that would have kept her in the living-room at that moment. She walked past Gareth, and up the stairs as if he weren't there, but inside her was the fierce primitive urge to hurt him as she had been hurt, and it needed all her strength of will to resist it.

She leaned trembling against her bedroom door, and heard the voices faintly from downstairs, Gareth's deeper tones, then her aunt's lighter ones in reply. She went to her bed and sat down, clasping her hands tightly together. And she waited for her aunt to come and tell her that Gareth was leaving Rhu-na-Bidh.

It seemed an age before she heard her aunt's voice floating up the stairs. 'He's gone. Come down and have something to eat.' Holly looked at her watch, surprised to see that a mere twenty minutes had passed. She walked slowly down, and her Aunt Margaret pushed a plate of toast at her as she went into the kitchen. 'Start on that. I'm doing scrambled egg.'

'But I couldn't eat a—'

'You'll eat, or you'll be ill.'

Holly sat on a stool, careful not to move it lest she trap a kitten. And suddenly she was reminded of Gareth's words, only recently, when he had spoken of his desire to buy his cottage. 'Is he going?' she asked.

'No,' her aunt looked at her, waiting, it seemed, for her protest.

Holly went numb. For a moment she couldn't speak, then, very carefully, she said: 'You mean – he w-won't?'

'No, love, I mean I've told him he can stay.'

'B-but—' Holly stammered, feeling a strange sensation of helplessness sweep over her. 'But – why? Why?'

'He offered to leave – he's very upset—' She stopped at Holly's choked gasp of disbelief. 'Yes, he is, strange as it may seem. But after we'd talked, I realized that I couldn't just let him go, like that. It wouldn't be right, no matter who he – or his father is. I know him as a man I can trust. I cannot send him away – for if I did it would be on my conscience for the rest of my life.'

'No!' Holly breathed. 'Then I must go.'

'You won't.' Aunt Margaret's voice had changed. There was that decisive note, the different tone she used with pupils, firmer, assured. And Holly looked at her, feeling something of that authority.

'You'll stay here too – for you're mine, and I cannot be on my own in the house this winter – I need the company. I'm getting old, Holly, and perhaps selfish, but please, I beg you, help me. The animals need you. Would you desert them because of one man, and thus further compound the wrong his father did?'

Slowly, doubtfully, Holly shook her head. 'I'll try. I will t-try,' she said at last, and Aunt Margaret smiled faintly as she put a plate of scrambled eggs before her.

'That will do for now,' she said. 'I love you, Holly, always remember that.'

Holly knew that she had to keep busy, to stop herself from thinking about Gareth. The pain of it all was so much more intense because of what had happened just before her discovery. She went to the stable to see to the animals after she had eaten. There was work to be done there, clearing out old straw, shaking and airing the blankets, and she set to, with all her energy. Her aunt's words just before she had left the house came back. Gareth had told Aunt Margaret that he and his father didn't get on; that he had left home because of their constant clashes, clashes which came from deep personality differences, that he didn't share his father's lust for power and money – Holly shuddered. It all sounded so pat – but then he had had all night to think out something. She clenched her teeth to stop herself from crying again. The time for that was over. The wonder that had so recently been hers, for such a short sweet time, was over too. She was filled with a cold implacable dislike for Gareth. Let him stay. He was hard and ruthless – traits which he shared with his father, even if he didn't know it. But his days of gloating were over. He had tried, however briefly, to make Holly see him as a man – had tried to make her love him. Love him . . . she touched her lips for a moment. Never again would he do that. Never. Perhaps it was fitting that he was here. Her mother's words came back to Holly again as she stood in the large dry barn. 'He is your enemy,' she had said. 'Remember, he killed your father.'

'I'll remember,' she said softly as she bent to stroke the Afghan, who lay clumsily at her feet, his huge paws catching her legs as he moved. Perhaps, soon, Gareth would want to leave. She remembered the first time she had seen him, here, at almost the same spot. She looked quickly towards the door as if he might be there, the tall, broad-shouldered, well-built gipsy she had distrusted immediately. She had felt the tingle of danger at the back of her neck then, when their hands had touched. It had been a warning – a true warning – and the reality of it had been much worse than she could have ever dreamed.

With tears pricking her eyelids, she turned and began sweeping the stone floor. Herbert lolloped to his feet, eager to help, and became entangled with the broom, nearly falling over.

'Oh, you silly dog!' Holly sighed, a reluctant smile refusing to be quashed. She helped the huge shaggy animal to his feet and he licked her hand gratefully.

'You're lovely really, aren't you?' she asked as she looked into his beautiful yellow eyes. 'Who would let you get lost, and not try to find you?'

There had been no word from Sergeant MacLeish, and he had promised to circulate the dog's description to all police stations in Scotland. It was a mystery where he had come from, a real mystery.

The days passed, and Holly began to realize that her aunt did need help. She was getting older, there was no denying that, and Holly was as fond of the animals as her aunt, and she enjoyed looking after them. It was something to do. Mike was attentive. They went out several times during the next few weeks, and he was more considerate than ever – truly, she thought, he was a nice man, a gentle person. He seemed determined to make her laugh, but there was affection there as well – affection she tried to return, but vainly. It was as if her heart was numb inside her, well anaesthetized after the disastrous encounter with Gareth. His name had not once been mentioned, except on their first date after Holly's heartbreaking discovery. She had told him briefly of her finding out Gareth's real identity, and was astonished to find Mike didn't know anything about it. He clicked his fingers after she had told him.

'That explains a lot,' he admitted, and she saw a hard line to his mouth. 'I'll bet Dad told Laura – she's dead keen, to put it mildly. And why not, if he's heir to a few million? Well, well.' He shook his head. 'An ordinary fellow doesn't stand a chance, does he?'

Holly tried to speak lightly. 'Apparently he likes the simple life. It might not suit Laura – living in the back-woods for ever.'

'Are you joking?' He slanted her a cynical glance. 'Wait till she's hooked him, then see. She'll have him away from here so fast that you won't see them for dust. I suppose he'll finish the book first, at least.'

'Book? What book?'

'Laura let it slip that he was writing a biography of his grandfather – apparently he was very fond of the old chap. She didn't say who he was or anything – of course, she wouldn't, if she's been sworn to secrecy, would she? But it came out by chance. She thinks it's mad, a waste of time – but he's dead serious about it.'

Holly was silent. So that explained his reason for not working – partly, anyway – and perhaps his walks at night. He would need to unwind if he was sitting at a desk for hours, researching and writing. A cold dislike swept through her. She didn't want to know anything about Gareth Greene – she knew enough already to last her a lifetime.

She changed the subject, and he wasn't mentioned again. And somehow, as the weeks passed, she found that she and Mike were reaching a pleasant under-standing. The relationship was undemanding. He needed someone to talk to as much as anything, and Holly was, although not lonely, glad of his pleasant companionship. They went out, they laughed, danced, ate together – and kissed. But the kisses were those of friends, not lovers, and Holly felt she knew the reason. Laura was still at Mike's home. She had gone away briefly, on an urgent modelling assignment, then come back. She was out with Gareth once or twice a week, although this Holly already guessed, by the frequency with which his Land-Rover left at night, sometimes not returning until one or two in the morning. No doubt, she thought bitterly, one night when she heard the quiet throb of the engine coming up the path at two o'clock, he was getting his money's worth. She put her hands to her ears to shut out the noise of the engine. How she hated him!

She saw little of him now. It was as if there was an unspoken agreement for them both to stay out of each other's way. If by chance he should come over to her aunt's when Holly was in – he usually waited until she was out, she knew – she would leave the room without speaking, and he would look at her with a return of his former arrogance on his features – a 'damn you' look, as if he no longer cared what she thought. Holly still occasionally had that primitive longing to scratch his eyes out, but it was fading with time, and she found she could even look through him without flinching.

The kittens had gone to homes in the village mainly, though one had found a home with Aunt Margaret's oldest and dearest friend, Eileen Macdonald, who lived alone ten miles away in a remote cottage something similar to Aunt Margaret's. Holly's aunt had been trying to persuade her to have a dog for a long time, but had compromised with a kitten.

'It's a start at least,' she sniffed. 'The little devil will be company for her in the winter, anyway. Though I don't know why she doesn't come and stay here over the worst months. I ask her every year, but she refuses – she's so stubborn.' Holly repressed a smile. The two old women were alike in so many ways, and Aunt Margaret was equally obstinate, but would never admit it.

Then one day, surprisingly, Eileen phoned. She had decided that a dog would be a good idea after all – and company for the kitten. Would Margaret pick a nice quiet one for her? Holly, who had answered the phone, assured Eileen that her aunt would be only too pleased, and that she would get her to ring back when she came home from the village.

Aunt Margaret was astounded, and immediately fell into a panic over which dog it would be. 'A nice quiet one – oh dear!' she put her hand to her face.

'What about little Speedy?' Holly suggested. He was so named because he was terribly lazy, a small rough-haired brown mongrel of indeterminate age. Holly had grown very fond of him, but knew Eileen would be a good mistress.

Her aunt nodded. 'You know, I think you're right,' she said. 'I'll take him now – before she changes her mind.'

Holly watched them leave with mixed feelings. It was one less mouth to feed – but she would miss him. She turned back with a sigh, and went indoors to finish the ironing.

Her aunt gave her a shock when she returned several hours later. Holly went quickly to the door on seeing her.

'Why, what is it?' she asked, seeing the worry on the older woman's kindly face.

'It's Eileen.' Aunt Margaret pulled off her cloak with a sigh, and flung it over the back of the settee. 'She's just getting over the 'flu, and she doesn't look at all well – and she fell last week and bruised her leg, so she's wandering about like a child. I made her sit down, and cooked her a meal. I insisted on her coming here for a week or two, but she wouldn't hear of it. Oh, dear,' she sat down heavily on a chair. 'I don't know *what* to do. She worries me terribly.'

There was a pause, and Holly bit her lip. She looked out of the kitchen window as she filled the kettle for tea. It was a bitterly cold November day, the air as brittle as glass, and with snow threatening. Not nice for an old woman living alone. . . . 'Why don't you go there for a couple of days, Aunt?' Holly turned and asked her quickly, before the impulse faded. 'I'll take care of the animals.'

'My dear! But would you – I mean – you know—' her aunt sighed heavily. 'How *sweet* of you, but—'

'I insist,' said Holly, and put the kettle on the gas.

'How wonderful of you,' and Aunt Margaret smiled as she bent to loosen her shoes. In fact she bent so quickly that Holly only glimpsed the smile briefly. And somehow it puzzled her.

Later, when she realized what she had done, she wondered if she had been foolish. But it was too late to change her mind. Aunt Margaret, showing an unusual turn of speed, had phoned Eileen straight away, had gone over to Gareth's to see if he would run her in the Land-Rover, '—it means you can use the Mini while I'm away. Of course it's only for a day or two, but I know you won't like to ask Gareth to run you, and my bike isn't very comfortable if you're not used to it—' There was no stopping Aunt Margaret in full flow, and Holly didn't attempt to. Of course, she reasoned to herself, a few days away with an old friend would do her aunt all the good in the world. She never had a holiday, never a day off – and Holly owed her so much, perhaps in a small way it would help towards repaying. She soon put the odd idea, that somehow Aunt Margaret had hoped she would offer, right out of her head . . .

The next morning, Holly said good-bye to her aunt in the living-room.

She hugged her. 'Don't worry about the animals,' she told her. 'I'll look after them properly, and—'

'—and Gareth will take them out at night. I've asked him.'

'You shouldn't have,' burst out Holly. 'I would—'

'It's too much for a girl alone. He doesn't mind. You don't have to *meet* him or anything.'

Holly was silent. The strangest thought crossed her mind. Laura wouldn't be pleased if he had to leave her to dash home . . . and the thought was oddly satisfying. She smiled and kissed the older woman.

'I'll phone every night and give you a report, don't worry. And you'll stay about a week?'

'Certainly no more,' Aunt Margaret assured her. 'But you know how stubborn old ladies are. They won't be told—' Muttering and grumbling, she eased herself into her cloak, and Holly smiled to herself. She watched them go, and something like a pang of regret assailed her. Had she been impulsive? Perhaps, but she had had no choice. It was the least she could do – and there was no need to even see that obnoxious, hateful man, let alone speak to him. She was fully independent, had the car if she needed to go to Kishard, and had everything to hand for the animals. No, there was no need at all to even be aware of his existence. She would invite Mike around too, for company, if she felt lonely. Yes, that would be nice. Thus reassured, Holly began to plan her day.

It was strange at first, being alone with no one to talk to, and it reminded Holly of her last few months before coming to her aunt's, when she had lived alone in her home until it was sold, after her mother had died. But now was different, she knew. There were the dogs and cats for company, and work to do, meals to prepare – and fires to keep going. The house was old, the walls very thick, and Aunt Margaret always kept two fires going in winter. One, in the living-room, was an open fire on which she burned coal or peat. That heated a back boiler so that there was constant hot water. The other was a coke burner in a corner of the kitchen which heated four radiators. Outside in the barn she kept two electric radiators for cold weather. They were expensive to run, but safer than any other form of heating, and Holly was reminded to go and switch them on full for the animals as she looked at her watch. Five o'clock, and Gareth had just come back from running her aunt to Eileen's. She had heard the Land-Rover door slam, then his front door, and her hands had tightened at her side. Just occasionally she was overcome with the wish that she were a man, so that she could exact justice in the most basic and physical way – with fists. The helpless feeling she had was worst of all, the sensation of being unable to do anything.

Angrily she turned away from the window and went out to the barn. The bitter cold caught her breath, and she looked up to a leaden sky, heavy and grey with no moon. She shivered. As she came out of the barn a few minutes later, it began to snow.

Holly phoned Mike later during the evening, and he came over. They spent a pleasant evening listening to the radio, talking, sitting by the large fire toasting their toes. Mike sighed. 'You know, Holly,' he said, 'you can't beat an open fire, can you? I could sit here all night just looking at it – but you can't do that with radiators. The only open fire we have is in the hall, and that's only for show.'

Holly laughed. 'I hope you don't think you're stopping here all night – even if it is only to watch the flames,' she said.

He shook his head. 'Uh-uh, you're safe enough with me – but I think you already know that, don't you? Not that I don't want—' he pulled her to him in a half joking, half serious movement, and kissed her gently, '—to kiss you,' he finished minutes later. 'But I'd hate to spoil this very nice friendship – and it would, wouldn't it, if I tried—' he stopped.

Holly turned a serious face towards him. 'Yes, it would,' she said quietly. 'I can't explain it, Mike, but I'm not ready for – for anything else yet.' But inside her was the memory of something that had nearly happened not so long ago, and she went warm.

Later, when Mike went, she stood in the porch waiting until his tail lights vanished down the track. Gareth's Land-Rover was parked in its usual place, and the light shone out from his front room.

The sky was still heavy with the snow it held, and there was a faint dusting on the ground, silver powder that glittered in the light from behind her. She breathed deeply of the clear cold air, and a strange wave of utter loneliness swept over her as she looked across involuntarily at his lighted window. Then, quickly, before she could think anything else, she went in and shut the door. She would take Smokey and Kazan out later, she decided – when there was no possibility of meeting *him*.

CHAPTER SIX

HOLLY should have known what had happened when she woke the next morning, for the light in the bedroom was so bright that she was awake an hour earlier than usual. She went to the window – then stopped in sheer amazement at the sight which met her eyes. Everywhere was dazzling white. The whole world for as far as she could see was blanketed in thick snow, and swirling flakes fell quickly down, ever down.

Pulling on her warm dressing-gown, she ran downstairs to let the animals out, and was met by a blank white wall when she opened the back door. The snow was at least three feet deep – and still falling, so fast that it was like a constant downwards blur in front of her eyes. The dogs took one look and turned back as if to say: 'Not on your life!' and she laughingly agreed with their expressions. They would have to *tunnel* their way through if they wanted to go out. She grimaced, patted Kazan's head absent-mindedly as he whined, and went to get dressed. A spade was always kept in the pantry. Holly knew she was in for some hard work. It was just as well her aunt had gone the previous day, she reflected as she donned warm sweater and trews. She would never have made it in this. The other, disquieting thoughts didn't come until later – much later. ... She had worked hard shovelling snow, and had cleared a good square patch outside the back door, sprinkling salt down before she went back indoors for a well-earned cup of tea, to stop the ceaseless snow from settling too easily. The animals were pushed – very reluctantly out, and she collapsed in a chair with a hot cup of tea by her side.

And then she realized the truth, and sat bolt upright, nearly knocking the tea over. She was well and truly marooned – with *Gareth*. The thought was so shocking that for a few moments she didn't move. The snow had cut them off just as surely as if they were stranded on a desert island in the middle of the sea. Holly had been at her aunt's previously when snow came, and had known the excitement at feeling isolated from civilization, the sensation of being cut off, cocooned in a warm house from the cold outside. But then she had been a child, protected from cares by adults, and it had been an adventure to savour. Now was different. She was the responsible one, and the animal's welfare was in her hands, as was the running of the house.

The thoughts were sobering. At eighteen Holly had had more than her fair share of unhappiness. This was another thing altogether. She knew somehow that it was a test. How she coped would be a measure of her independence as a young adult. And the thought came irresistibly: Gareth will expect me to need help. At that she sat up straighter in her chair, and drank the refreshing tea. 'I'll be damned if I will,' she said aloud. Then she stood up and went to the phone. The first job was to reassure Aunt Margaret, who would be equally marooned – and undoubtedly worried at leaving her niece and the animals.

Her aunt was much relieved at Holly's carefree reassurances that everything was, and would be, well under control. 'My dear child,' she moaned, 'if I'd imagined this! Are you sure? The tinned animal food is in the pantry—'

'I know where everything is,' Holly laughed. 'Honestly! If the worst comes to the worst, I'll start making bread in a day or two – er – where's the recipe?'

'In the sideboard, written on the back cover of a knitting book – I think – oh, dear—'

'Don't worry! I've got a good idea anyway. I'll find it. Now, you go and look after Eileen. Give her my love. I'll ring tonight. Good-bye, love.'

She put down the phone thoughtfully. She had been joking about making bread – but somehow, looking out at the swirling white world outside, she wondered. The joke might yet come true.

Two days passed. The snow was now six feet deep, and Holly had made a path to the barn which kept getting obscured by more falls. Gareth had been hard at work too – and although they had had no direct confrontation, it had been a near thing once or twice. The world was a completely different place, devoid of sound, save perhaps for the occasional harsh cry of a gull as it quested vainly for food away from the sea. There might have been no one else living. It was an eerie sensation, and Holly was glad that the phone was still working. Then, on Sunday, nearly a week after her aunt had gone, she picked it up to ring Mike, and it was dead. She rattled the receiver rest vainly, knowing that it was useless even as she did so. It was a miracle the lines hadn't come down before. She replaced the phone thoughtfully and went to the front door. Sunday, and the world was silent. She shivered suddenly, feeling cold and lost, then went in and shut the door. And now she knew true loneliness.

The day dragged interminably. Holly had read nearly all the books in the house, and went up to the spare bedroom in the afternoon, to see if there were any magazines worth reading. The painful memory of what had happened as a result of her last visit there tugged achingly at her heart as she went in, and she avoided looking towards the pile of *Sunday Times* which still lay there. If only she had selected some others. If – if . . . But there were no ifs any more. She knew the truth, and it had hurt – but now the pain was lessening. In its place was something else, a deeper ache that Holly couldn't understand, and thought she never would. There she was wrong.

She went to feed the dogs a short while later. This was a job she enjoyed, and she always spent some time with them in the barn after they had eaten. The Afghan had settled in beautifully. A gentle dog for all his size, his only wish was to please, and Holly silently prayed that he would find a good home soon. She left them at last, shutting the door, leaving them free in the barn to play. There were occasional scraps, but nothing serious. It was, she reflected, as she made a cautious way across the slippery path she had carved, as if Aunt Margaret's influence still lingered, even when she was miles away, and they didn't want to do anything to displease her.

It was growing towards night. Stars shone faintly in a clear dark sky, and the air was crisp and sharp. And she was going to spend another evening alone . . . And then Holly saw a movement at Gareth's front door and turned her head slightly to avoid seeing him – and trod on a patch of ice. Brittle black ice, invisible to the keenest eye, but perhaps she would have managed to avoid it, save that the sight of that man had jerked her momentarily from her careful tread. She felt the ground slide sickeningly away from beneath her, heard, as if from a great distance, the metallic clatter as one of the plates she carried landed on the iron hard cobblestone, felt roughness beneath her side as she skidded helplessly along. The next moment she opened her eyes to stars twinkling benignly down at her, and a white wall of hard-packed snow at either side of her body.

For a few seconds she lay there, winded, wondering what had happened. Then, gasping, remembering, she tried to sit up. She had seen *him*. She didn't want him coming over. Struggling to her feet, she made her trembling way to the house, seeing it looming nearer, and it was jerking crazily as she struggled, her breathing quick and shallow to avoid the terrible pain down the left side of her body. And there was the taste of blood in her mouth . . .

She pushed open the door with a trembling hand, and almost fell into the living-room. She had to lean against the settee for a minute as pain and black nausea receded and came back in strong, frightening waves. The entire left side of her body, from shoulder to ankle, was one mass of harsh, intense, unbearable pain – and her arm – she knew it was bleeding by the sticky warmth of her sweater sleeve. Ignoring the two whining dogs who had come over to her, Holly dragged herself out to the kitchen and leaned over the sink. Slowly, using her right hand only, she began to ease her sweater off. At least it was red, she thought, choking back a sob. The blood wouldn't show . . .

She gritted her teeth as the last, painful part came. Just as she carefully pulled the sweater sleeve down her arm, she heard the front door open softly. But the sound didn't register, so engrossed was she with her task, until Gareth's voice came: 'Let me help.'

Gasping with shock, she turned partly round, feeling the blood leave her face. 'Go away!' she managed to say.

But he came slowly, inexorably forward and stopped beside her. Holly held the sweater to her instinctively, but it was an effort. Dislike mingled with embarrassment and pain, and she could scarcely speak, but she looked up at him, tried, and swayed like a reed. Shock had made her go faint.

'You're hurt.' His voice had a harsh tone to it. 'Let me help you. You must—'

'No.' But she could scarcely get the word out, and started to shiver helplessly in case he would touch her. Her legs began to buckle beneath her as she felt the pain in her left arm. 'Go – away—' she began, in a mere whisper of sound.

With a wordless exclamation he swung her up in his arms and carried her to the settee in front of the fire. Then he knelt before her. 'Listen to me, Holly. I'm going to get you some brandy. But first you need a blanket round you. Where is one?'

'In the bedding chest in my bedroom – under the window.' Tears of pain sprang to her eyes. She was too weak to fight any more. She watched him go, heard him returning down the stairs, two at a time, then he was in the room, holding a fluffy, brightly patterned Dutch blanket before the fire for several moments before draping it round her shoulders. The next second she was alone. And then she had time to think about what had happened. She closed her eyes tiredly. She couldn't struggle any more, the pain was too intense, and she was weak and tired – and blood filled her mouth with its salt taste, and trickled down her chin, and she wondered why . . .

'All right. Just hold that to your mouth for a minute.' The voice came in waves of sound, and she felt a cool damp flannel being pressed into her hand. Silently Holly obeyed, then waited for further instruction. It was easier, much easier not to argue.

'It's all right – you must have bitten your lip when you fell. It's nearly stopped now. Drink this. It might sting a little.'

She took the glass from him, sipped the rich warm brandy, felt it go down, making her cough a little. Then she handed the glass back, not looking at him. She didn't *want* to look at him. Maybe, in a minute, he would go away. Maybe . . .

'Now, let me have a look at your arm—' and as she flinched and tried to move away, tried to pull the blanket closer to her breast, he added harshly: 'I'm not looking at you, don't worry. I only want to see what you've done to your arm.' And he knelt down beside the settee and very gently took her left wrist in his hand and pulled it slightly away from her side.

The brandy had done something good to Holly. Although she still ached solidly, the shock of the alcohol had cleared her muzzy head, and she watched him as with swift fingers and a skilful detachment, he examined her bare arm. The blood on the long graze was dry, and the skin alongside it red and tender. He was bending forward so that she saw the top of his head and just a fraction of the dark face below it; his hair was very black in the light, glossy as a raven's wing, and as untidy as ever, as if he didn't care when he was alone, for he had not shaved either for several days, and she couldn't see the lower half of his face for beard. He was dressed in dark blue sweater and old jeans, his shoulders were broad and powerful . . . Hastily she turned her head away, before he should look up and catch her, and he mistook the movement.

'Did I hurt you?' he asked. She had to look at him then, to answer, and his dark eyes, indifferent as a stranger's, watched her as she answered: 'No. It hurts anyway. I haven't broken it, have I?'

He shook his head, and a lock of hair escaped and fell over his forehead. She had the absurd urge to flick it back – and stiffened at the thought.

'No, at least I don't think so. You've a bad graze – and you'll be sore as hell tomorrow. The bruises are already coming out. How's your leg?'

'They hurt,' she answered briefly. What are we doing like this – talking? she thought. She didn't want *this*. 'I'll be all right soon,' she said slowly. 'Thank you for the brandy, and your h-help. I'll manage now.'

He stood up and looked down at her. A glint that might almost have been amusement showed in his eyes for a moment before vanishing Then he said very carefully and concisely, as if she were deaf, or stupid, she thought wildly: 'You won't manage at all. There's nothing else for it – I'll have to move in here. You can't be alone now.'

At her violent movement of protest he smiled grimly. 'I've no more desire to come than you to have me,' he said. 'But I have no choice. I wouldn't even leave a dog in the condition you're in.'

Holly struggled to her feet, finding a desperate kind of strength.

'I don't want you.' Her eyes blazed into his. 'Don't you understand?'

His eyes narrowed. 'You've made *that* perfectly clear – I'd have to be pretty thick not to know. But I suggest you call a truce for a few days—' he glanced briefly at the window '—or more.' His eyes were that dark unfathomable, *frightening* black as he looked at her again. 'And you don't need to have any old-fashioned ideas about the propriety of the situation. I promise I won't rape you—' she gasped sharply at the bald word, heard him continue: 'In fact, I have no desire to touch you at all, so you're quite safe.'

'How dare you say such things!' she protested, and some of the life came back into her.

He lifted a cynical eyebrow. 'Let's cut out the outraged modesty – it doesn't go well nowadays, and you're no Victorian miss, so don't put on the act.'

'You're hateful!' she whispered.

'Yes, I am,' he agreed. 'And we've been all over *that* before, too. I suggest we skip it. I'll go and get my things and damp my fire down. You'd better think about where I'm going to sleep. I won't be long.' He turned and walked towards the door, then paused before opening it. 'I'll dress your arm when I return.' Then he was gone.

It was the strangest thing, she thought, but gradually it was as if Gareth was assuming control, taking over. And there was nothing she could do about it, that was the awful part. It was later that evening. Holly sat – as best she could – on the settee. Gareth had bandaged her arm, after bathing it, and some of the pain had subsided. It was now the rest of her which ached, especially her left hip and leg. It was extremely difficult for her to move, and she had to grit her teeth every time she did so, so that no involuntary cry of pain would escape.

But at least now she was on her own for a few precious minutes. Gareth had gone to attend to the dogs in the barn. They were no longer able to have a run at night, merely a scamper round the wire-netted area, which he had painstakingly cleared for them. They loved the snow, that much Holly already knew, and dived and rolled in it joyfully, much the same as children would.

He had returned shortly after leaving her before, with a pile of clothes and a couple of towels, and had said: 'Which room?'

Through frozen lips Holly had answered: 'You'd better have my aunt's. I changed the bedding the morning she left.'

'Right.' And he'd gone up, whistling as if nothing was amiss. Holly had clenched her fists, willing herself to be better, wishing it hadn't happened. The sooner she was able to move freely, the sooner he would go. That prospect seemed infinitely attractive, and yet . . . and yet strangely something stirred now inside her, some deeply buried emotion she couldn't begin to unravel at the thought that he would be living here, sleeping only feet away from her, eating, working – Holly put her hand to her face in quick dismay. What's the matter with me? she thought. What on earth am I thinking of? And there was no one to answer her, and only her heightened colour to betray her thoughts.

She looked deep into the glowing fire and tried to ease herself more comfortably into position, wincing with pain.

Then as she heard the porch door opening, the heavy stamp of Gareth's boots, she hastily stopped moving. She heard them drop to the stone floor, then the door opened, and with him came a blast of cold air, quickly dispelled as he shut the door behind him.

'They're all settled down for the night.' He came over towards the fire. 'It's freezing out. Those radiators are on full blast in the barn, and it's still cold.'

She looked up at him standing rubbing his hands in front of the fire. It wasn't so difficult somehow for her to talk about the dogs.

'There's nothing we can do,' she answered. 'They'll sleep together in a huddle by them if it gets really cold.'

He nodded absentmindedly, as if already he was thinking of something else. The silence grew brittle, and Holly stirred uneasily. She saw his crooked smile, as if he guessed her unease, then he said:

'You must have a bath tonight – not too hot – plenty of salts in. Have you some?'

'Yes,' she answered. 'But how will—' She stopped.

'How will you manage?' he inquired dryly. 'Very well, I should imagine – especially if you bear in mind that if you get stuck you'll have to shout for me to help you.'

She looked up sharply, hating his tone, the dry cynicism, and her voice was hard as she answered him. 'Don't worry, it's not likely.'

He laughed, but there was little humour in it. 'It *was* a joke.'

'I don't find it very amusing.'

'No? You wouldn't, though, would you?' And she saw that he was angry, and it was obscurely frightening. What was she to make of him, this tough, powerful man who stood there settling himself in, quite at home in her aunt's house – and against whom she felt so powerless in so many different ways? There were greater depths to him, she realized, than anyone knew, and it was oddly disturbing.

Not for the first time, Holly experienced a strange breathless feeling, as if she was going to faint. She turned her head away quickly, not wanting him to see any weakness, however slight, for it would be a weapon in his hands – and he had more than enough already. They were stranded, alone in a world of white, no contact with anyone else – and now the realization came upon her with sweeping intensity that filled her being in a huge tidal wave. There were just the two of them, together in the house – *together*. And there was nothing that she could do about it, no way of persuading him to leave, for he was determined to stay, and she knew without any need of being told that his will was implacable.

He looked at his watch. 'I suggest you have your bath now. Have you any liniment?'

'Yes, I think so.' Holly bit her lip. It was no use trying to fight him. It would be much easier to do what she was told. She struggled to get to her feet, and when he leaned over to help her, did not resist. His hand was light and firm on her good arm, and when she stood, she gathered the blanket more tightly round her with a dignity that was oddly touching. 'Thank you,' she said. 'I'll go up now.'

'Yes. Let me run the water for you,' he said, watching.

She lifted her chin. 'I'll manage – thank you.' It was going to be agony to walk, she knew, but she would do it – she *would*.

'And don't lock the door.'

'What?' Alarm flared in her, and she paused in her agonizing struggle to the stairs, and turned, eyes wide.

'I mean, for if you do get stuck. Don't worry, I promise I'll be down here *all the time*.'

She saw a muscle tighten in his cheek, and turned away without another word. Of course it was sensible, but . . .

Painfully she made her way up the stairs. And later, as she lay in the warm, salts-softened water, she thought over things. She was too weak to resist Gareth, she knew. Better now, for the time being, to let him act as he was, deciding things, looking after her. That he was capable and efficient she had no doubt. She must, she knew, try to put to one side the overwhelming distaste she felt in his presence. Compromise, I'll just have to compromise, she decided – and suddenly thought of her mother. What would she say if she were here? she wondered, and tears sprang to her eyes. She won't be, ever again, she thought, and in a way, that is because of his father too. And she wondered if her mother had known that Neville Greene had a son. Holly could not know that soon her question would be answered, startlingly and most shockingly.

The next morning when Holly woke up, she was almost completely unable to move for several moments. She lay there panic-stricken, feeling as if she had been run over by a steamroller, and then slowly and painfully reached out her right arm to try and lever herself up. The faint liniment smell arose as she stifled a cry of sheer agony. She had rubbed herself well after the bath, then put on her oldest pyjamas and gone to bed, after shouting down to Gareth that she was safely out. She would compromise, oh yes, she would do *that*, because she didn't have much choice – but it didn't mean she had to go down and sit by the fire with him as if they were old friends.

Now, sitting at the side of the bed, she began, slowly and painfully, to pull on her dressing-gown. She was thirsty, and the bedroom was cold, and she didn't care if he was downstairs, she was going down in her dressing-gown because the prospect of getting clothes on was too daunting to face – yet.

Slowly, one cautious agony-filled step at a time, holding tightly to the rail, Holly made her way down. All was quiet. Even the dogs were still asleep by a dead fire. They roused themselves to greet her gently, sensing her pain, and she made her way to the kitchen, which was cold and empty. Suddenly the thought came – what if he had changed his mind and gone home? And oddly it made her feel lonely. She shook off the feeling irritably. What on earth's the matter with me? she thought crossly. I don't want him here anyway – and yet . . . and she suddenly remembered the previous night. He had brought her up a cup of cocoa and two aspirins, and knocked at the bedroom door just as she was sliding carefully between the sheets. When she had answered, he had brought it in, told her to take the pills, said good night, and gone, shutting the door quietly behind him. Holly had felt a twinge of something approaching remorse – absurd, of course – but for just a moment, as she had thanked him for the cocoa, there had been a look in his eyes that had made her heart skip a beat. A bleak, almost lonely look.

Now she put the kettle on the gas and waited for it to boil, turned on the grill for toast, and the kitchen began to warm. After letting the dogs and cats out she brewed tea, reached out for a cup, and hesitated. Putting the cup on the level working surface, she poured milk into it, and her heart began to beat faster. Should she? She didn't want to, but – hesitantly, biting her lip, Holly reached out for another beaker and put milk and sugar in it. It was the very least she could do, she knew, and yet . . .

'Oh, don't be stupid!' she told herself, and before she could change her mind, poured tea into the beaker, slipped two pieces of bread under the grill and turned it low, and set off back on the incredibly long trek to her aunt's bedroom.

She knocked and waited, suddenly regretting her impulse ...

'Come in,' a sleep-blurred voice answered, and she swallowed hard and turned the handle to open the door. Gareth lay in her aunt's fourposter, and it was strange to see anyone other than Aunt Margaret there. He was nearly awake, sprawled out on his stomach, one arm on the pillow, the other hanging down.

He muttered something inaudible, and she crept softly to the bedside table, intent now on getting out before he woke properly.

'A – a cup of tea,' she said quietly, almost in a whisper.

He pulled himself round suddenly, making her jump, so tense was she. She put the cup down, trying not to look at him – trying not to see the dark blue pyjamas that were now visible as he struggled into a sitting position rubbing his face to wake himself up. Against that white background of pillow and sheets he looked darker and more gipsyish than ever, and Holly found herself powerless to look away. There was something physically magnetic about him, and his eyes caught and held hers, and she stood as if mesmerized. His pyjama jacket was undone, there didn't appear to be any buttons on it, revealing his chest, thickly covered with black hair rising to a powerful neck above which his puzzled face surveyed her. He spoke, and the spell was broken. '*You* brought me tea?'

'Yes.' She turned away lest he should see her face,

for it would betray her. Then suddenly she smelled burning – and her hand went to her cheek. 'The toast – I've forgotten the toast – oh!' She fumbled for the handle and went out, leaving the door open in her agitation, and made her painful way downstairs. Even as she grabbed the grill pan and flung the blackened smoking pieces of bread out, she knew relief that it had happened. She sat down shaking, for coming downstairs had been agonizing – and more. She knew that if she had stayed a moment, just one second longer, in that bedroom, Gareth would have known the truth – and what would he have made of *that*? She had to put her hand out for support on the kitchen table. She thought she hated him, she knew she should – yet now, only minutes before, as she had watched him rouse himself from sleep, seen the oddly gentle expression on his face as he woke – seen too the surprise in his eyes as he saw the tea, she knew that nothing had changed. Despite everything, her treacherous heart had told her what her mind had refused to admit. She had wanted to go and hold him, and feel his arms around her. Whether it was love or mere physical attraction, she didn't know, she was too confused – but she had ached to have him kiss her.

Holly poured herself out a cup of tea with trembling hands, and drank it down quickly. I'm going mad, she thought. I hate everything he stands for, and is, and yet here I am, shaking like a leaf at the thought of him. Oh, wouldn't he be delighted to know *that*! He had made no secret of the fact that he found Laura irresistible – he must be missing her and all she could give him. Holly closed her eyes, feeling again a surge of the old jealousy she had thought dead. Oh, yes, Laura would be furious at being snowed up, so near – and yet so far. And Gareth must be, equally so. Holly had no illusions about him, in spite of her shameful longing for him. A rich man's son, clearly he had had no difficulty in ever getting everything he wanted in life. He had promised not to touch Holly – she still went warm at the thought of the blunt way he had expressed himself – but perhaps, after a few days of being alone with her, he might feel differently, might be tempted to try . . . She drew herself up sharply. What on earth was she doing, thinking like this? Holly hastily cut more bread and put it under the grill. The last loaf, and nearly finished. Today she would have to find the recipe and make some, and it would be something to do, for now, she realized, life was going to be difficult, very difficult indeed . . .

Gareth lit both fires when he came down, and Holly told him she was planning to make bread. She found it hard to speak naturally now, feeling as she did, and he looked briefly at her as if he too sensed something, but didn't understand it.

'You want any help?' he asked.

'Please. W-when I have to leave the dough to rise in the hearth. The tins are heavy.'

He nodded. 'Just tell me when. I'll go and let the dogs out now, then I'm going home for some things. May I work in the bedroom?'

She looked quickly at him. 'It's cold up there. What sort of work do you mean?'

'Writing,' he answered briefly, almost aggressively, as if waiting for her comment.

'Oh! Well, you can do it in the living-room. It's warmer. I – I'll keep out of your way – there's lots to do in the kitchen.'

He looked round in disbelief, then shrugged. 'All

right. I'll take the table under the window – that'll be out of your way anyway. I'll bring some food over as well. How's the milk situation?'

'I'm using powdered, but there are plenty of tins of evaporated in the pantry. Why?'

He shrugged again. 'I've got some as well. I just wondered.'

He had shaved, combed his hair back, and looked, Holly realized with a sharp hurtful pang, very attractive. But she mustn't – she must try not to think of him as a man. As he walked out of the front door, tall, broad-backed with his insolent gipsy walk, she watched him go. And that will be rather difficult, she thought wryly. How could anyone ignore the physical presence of a man like *him* – a man like Gareth, who had, during a few brief sweet hours not so long ago, before she found out the truth, roused her to a vivid awareness of herself as a woman. She took a deep breath, felt the pain in her side mingling with that other, bitter, pain of treachery and rejection – for he had only been playing with her, she knew that now. And that talk of being unable to get out of going out with Laura – Holly shuddered helplessly. What a fool she had so nearly been! Perhaps it had been a good thing to have found out when she had about him. At least she had kept her self-respect, not gone completely overboard.

She turned angrily away from the door, running her good hand through her thick wavy hair. The house was warm again, the air outside crystal clear, and achingly beautiful, with the snow hard and glittery in the sun. And everything was so quiet . . . With an abrupt movement, she switched on the radio. The strains of the latest pop tune blared out, and she turned it down slightly. Then she went over to the table by the window, and moving gingerly, began to clear the accumulated debris of months from it and on to the windowsill. She heard crunching steps outside, and in a panic, moved too quickly with a pile of books. They crashed to the ground, and she tried to bend and pick them up – and nearly fainted in the wave of intense blinding pain that followed.

'What on earth—' she heard his angry exclamation as if from a great distance as she tried to straighten. He dropped a week-end case on to the table, then turned to her. His hands came out to hold her as she swayed, gasping, said: 'I was trying to get the table—'

'You little fool! You're in no condition to do anything. Can you move?'

'No – just l-leave me a moment.' She was pulsatingly aware of his nearness as she felt his hands at her waist, steadying her, gentle hands, almost caressing, not hard— 'Help me,' she cried softly, not knowing why, only that it was a plea for more than just help – it was a cry from her heart.

She heard his voice, soft, almost kind: 'Don't try and move yet, just stay there a moment.'

'Yes. Yes, I will.' They were still by the table, and he was imperceptibly nearer, instinctively trying to shield her as if with his own body. Only inches away, his hands warm and strong on her, and she felt the pain recede, only to be replaced by an ache equally intense – and much more disturbing. With a little sigh she leaned against him, felt rather than heard his heavy heartbeat, steady – not as slow as it should be – and her whole body tingled at the contact. His touch was fire, his breath was on her face, his own so near that if she looked up – her own heartbeats quickened, and suddenly he was moving, pushing her away. In a harsh voice he said: 'You'd better sit down, hadn't you?' The tension crackled in the room like fire, and with a wordless exclamation of pain she pushed his hands away and stumbled to the settee. He remained where he was, looking at her with dark shadowed eyes as he said abruptly: 'I'd better look at your arm again.'

'Don't trouble yourself,' she answered. 'I can do it.'

'Like hell you can!' He strode out into the kitchen and Holly was left on the settee, looking into the fire, her mind a turmoil of jumbled emotions. Pain, self-loathing – and worse, a tingling kind of excitement that both disturbed and frightened her. He had not been immune – she knew that as surely as if he had said it. But he hadn't needed to put it into words, for some things are so primitive that no words are necessary.

He seemed angry when he came back with the first-aid box. Silently he laid everything out, and she saw the muscle working in his jaw as he set about his self-appointed task. Without a word he gestured to her arm, and Holly rolled up the sleeve of the loose warm sweater she had chosen because of its comfort. As he bent, she said, unable to bear the oppressive silence a moment longer: 'You don't have to make it so obvious that you find your work distasteful. I said I could manage.'

'*Shut up!*' he said it without looking up, and for a moment she didn't believe her ears, then, as she realized, she jerked her arm angrily away from him.

'Don't bother,' she grated. '*Thanks.*'

'Don't be stupid.' He looked up then, and she was startled by the smouldering depths to his eyes. 'Listen,' he said. 'If you were a man I'd probably have belted you by now. But you're not, so I can't – therefore you'll just have to forgive the odd insult that slips out when I can't help it.'

She was completely silenced. She took a deep breath, about to say something, then thought better of it, and subsided. So now, at last, she knew what he *really* thought. Tears of pain and self-pity sprang to her eyes, and her lips trembled. He looked up, then said:

'Oh, for pity's sake, not tears now! All right, I'm sorry I told you to shut up. It was unbearably rude, and I humbly beg your forgiveness.'

The sarcasm in his voice made it worse. Holly gasped helplessly, hating him. 'I w-wish I *was*,' she stammered, when she could speak.

He looked up tight-lipped from his deft un-bandaging. 'Wish you were what?'

'A m-man! I'd like to p-punch you one,' and she meant it.

He swiftly unwound the last few inches of bandage and turning, flung it on the fire. His smile was twisted, no trace of humour in it, as he reached out for the new roll beside him. 'You'd just better be grateful you're not. You wouldn't stand a chance when I got going.'

'I suppose you imagine that violence solves everything,' she ground out bitterly, feeling helpless and weak. 'Is that how you sort out your problems – by fighting?'

'I have on odd occasions – but no, I don't believe in violence, oddly enough. There *are* times when a fight is justified, though.'

Holly winced slightly as he smeared ointment on her arm, then bandaged it. He looked sharply at her. 'You know,' he said, and his temper seemed to have cooled slightly, 'you talk like a real tough female, but you're not, are you?' He looked at her lashes, still damp and spiky with tears. 'Look at you. You still fall back on the oldest feminine weapon of all when the chips are down – tears, and a trembling mouth. Oh boy, oh boy! It never fails, does it?'

'You seem to know,' she rejoined. 'But then I dare say you've had lots of experience.'

He gave a short dry laugh. 'I don't go around making girls cry, if that's what you mean.'

Holly would never know what made her say the next words. That old urge to hurt him perhaps. But she was to regret them. Almost without thinking, she shot back: 'Girls will put up with a lot when they're going out with a millionaire's son.'

She saw the quick closing of his expression, the tightening of his jaw. He stood up. Every word was hard and concise. 'I didn't notice *you* holding back that night in the Land-Rover – and you didn't know I'd got money then, did you?' Then, after a pause, he added softly: 'I might have done a lot better, who knows?'

Holly shrank back from the force in his words, the scorn he lashed her with, and unable to bear it, she cast her eyes down to the hand in her lap. Slowly she tightened it into a fist. But she said nothing. At eighteen, she was no match for this tall angry man threatening her with his words of contempt. With a little shudder she stood up and went shakily away from him – up the stairs and into her bedroom, there to lie down, tears of tiredness and weakness filling her eyes and blurring the room so that everything danced crazily round. She curled up in the cold bed, and, sunk in pain and despair, tried to sleep.

Eventually she did, and had vague troubled dreams, in which she was lost in the snow and couldn't find home. She stirred uneasily as she heard a voice from far away calling her name, then, feeling a touch on her arm, woke instantly.

Gareth was standing by the bed. She looked at him, then weakly closed her eyes. 'Please go away,' she begged.

'No. Come down. It's too cold up here. I've made a meal, and it's ready. Aren't you hungry?'

The smouldering anger was gone, and that was a relief. Holly knew she could not have taken any more. Her nerves were ragged, her whole body sharply, vividly awake to this man's every word – and she couldn't face it. She wanted peace and quiet, for the beginnings of delayed shock were making her feel tired and light-headed. She struggled to sit up, and began to shiver. 'I am hungry,' she admitted. 'But I don't w-want to—' and she stopped, frightened, trembling.

He said softly: 'The fighting's over, Holly. I've been trying to – I didn't realize how ill you were. I'm sorry.' And in this apology there was no sarcasm. 'Come now.'

He helped her out of the bed, and she began walking to the door. He caught her as she stumbled. 'Gently does it. Take it steady.'

His touch was impersonal, like a doctor's, and they made their way down, into the warm living-room. She looked at the clocks with their different times, did a quick deduction and said, astonished: 'It's nearly three o'clock.'

'Yes. You slept for hours. I brought you a hot water bottle. Didn't you notice?'

Surprised, she looked at him. 'I was holding one when I woke, but I didn't remember – was that you?'

'There's no one else here.' He looked round, pretending alarm. 'Is there?'

Holly shook her head, accepting the fact that he was trying – for some reason she couldn't fathom – to be pleasant.

'Thank you,' she told him. She looked over to the table by the window. It was transformed, with typewriter, piles of paper, and several opened books, and what looked like letters, scattered about. The table's previous contents – mainly books and vases – were stacked neatly along the windowsill. The typewriter had a sheet of paper in it, and there was an air of industry about the table, which now resembled a desk.

He saw the direction of her glance and said: 'I'll stop now you're down.'

'No, please don't,' she answered. 'Really. I'll sit by the fire if I may.' Then she remembered something. 'Oh – the bread. I must—'

'No need.' He touched her arm lightly and pointed to the hearth where three large tins rested, lightly covered with crisp clean tea-towels. Holly blinked, disbelieving, then knelt carefully and lifted up a corner of one towel. Even that was too much effort, and she gasped as she rose to her feet. 'That's—'

'Steady.' He pulled her down on the settee. 'Don't do *anything*. I mean it. You're suffering from shock, and you'll be ill if you're not careful.'

Numbly she nodded. She was completely drained of energy, and every movement was an effort. She knew the truth of his words, knew too, instinctively, that he meant what he said. The fighting was over – at least for a day or two.

'How did you find the recipe?' she asked.

He came to stand in front of her, one arm casually on the high mantelpiece. For a moment his dark eyes rested on her, then he said: 'I didn't. I mean – not your aunt's. I've made it before – and I remembered.' And he smiled.

'Oh, I see.' She took a deep breath to steady herself. Anything that concerned his life before he came to Rhu-na-Bidh was always disturbing to her, now more so. To change the subject quickly, she asked him: 'Did you say there was something to eat?'

'Yes. Sorry, I'll get it. Want a tray?'

'No, thanks.' She watched him go out to the kitchen, and felt her tense, aching body relax – very slightly. If there was a truce, and it seemed so, things would be easier now. For she sensed very strongly that he was making a great effort to keep his volatile temper leashed. She had borne the brunt of it several times – the last one so very recently. She knew just how powerful that temper could be – knew too, suddenly, that she was safe, at least until she was better.

Holly gave a little smile as she heard the clatter of plates, a muttered oath, and then the metallic sound of the cutlery drawer. He was trying, so she must try too. She sank her head back against the cushions of the comfortable settee. And it suddenly came to her that there was something extremely charming about Gareth – when he chose. She had seen glimpses of it before, of course, mainly with her aunt, and the evening at the Colonel's, but there had been little between the two of them – yet just then, as he had spoken about the bread, she had seen it again; a slow glinting kind of humour – essentially kind, almost gentle. Holly's heart thudded. It was no use thinking like this. It was bad enough fighting against her treacherous heart without allowing herself the painful luxury of watching for his mannerisms. She looked up as he came in carrying a plate on a tray.

'You'll have to have it on this, I'm afraid,' he began. 'The plate's as hot as – very hot. I burnt my hand.'

'I know. I heard.' She smiled slightly. 'Is it bad?'

'My hand, or my cooking?' He set the tray on her knee. 'Take your time. There's coffee after.'

She looked down at the steaming plate. On it were mashed potatoes, carrots, and rich looking chunks of meat in gravy. She looked up again, astonished. 'I didn't expect anything like this.'

'No? It's all out of tins – except the spuds. I managed those unaided. Well, eat up. Nearly time for the bread to go in.' He knelt and looked at the swollen dough, prodded it experimentally with a finger, said: 'Mmm, yes,' then picked up two tins and went out.

Holly began to eat the food, which was delicious, and found she was extremely hungry. She could not stop watching him however as he returned. It wasn't her imagination. He was making an effort to be nice, and the difference in him was remarkable. It was as if the tension that sparked inevitably between them when they were together was switched off. She found this fact oddly warming; perhaps, she thought, as she ate her dinner, perhaps he'll wait until I'm better, and then – She swallowed a piece of carrot the wrong way, and had to cough. That's it, she decided, when she could breathe again – he thinks I'm ill, and even *he* has to draw the line somewhere.

She looked down at her plate as Gareth came in for the last tin. At least, she thought wryly, it gives me a breathing space. And she carefully speared a succulent chunk of steak with her fork, quite unaware of the picture she made, her face pale and washed of all colour, the fine bones accentuated with the dark richness of her hair framing it. She looked beautiful and fragile, and it would have taken much more of a brute than Gareth Greene to be harsh with her. Nor did she see his eyes rest briefly on her for a moment from the kitchen doorway, see the softening of that gipsy hardness as he gazed at her, the imperceptible tightening of the muscles of his cheek before he spoke, and asked her if she wanted some fruit. If she had seen, she would not have understood the look, for Gareth was not a man to reveal his inner feelings. Yet for a moment they had showed, but only the smouldering blackness of his eyes was left afterwards as she looked up to answer him.

'No, thanks. But I'd like a coffee, please.'

'It's nearly ready.' He reached out and switched on the orange shaded lamp in the corner. 'It's getting too dark to see. I think there'll be more snow – it said so on the radio.'

'Oh no!' she looked up in dismay. 'How awful! As if we didn't have enough. Oh, what will we do?' She turned and looked out of the window.

'It is pretty grim. But there's nothing we *can* do, except stick it out – is there?'

She looked at him. 'Sometimes helicopters fly overhead, dropping bales of food to sheep on the mountains. People make S.O.S.s in the snow if they're desperate.'

He smiled slightly. 'But we're not. In fact, I'd say this place is more comfortable than most – thanks to your wonderful aunt. I'll bet the Colonel's finding it strange. He's not been here long.'

'And Laura—' then she stopped, realizing instinctively that this was not what she had meant to say.

What would he think? She added hastily: 'I mean, she's not used to it, is she? C-coming from London, I m-mean—' and her voice tailed away miserably as she waited for the blast of anger that would undoubtedly shatter the fragile but by now strangely welcome truce.

'No, she's not. Excuse me – I'll fetch the coffee.' It hadn't happened. He had not turned on her with sarcasm. She let out her breath in a tremulous sigh. He really *was* trying very hard. She put the tray aside. She couldn't eat any more now – but what she had eaten had been good.

When he brought in two beakers, Holly thanked him, and he looked at the plate. 'You don't eat enough, you know,' he commented. 'You'll have to try harder or you won't get well.'

'I'll try.' Holly felt suddenly embarrassed. She traced a pattern with her finger on the beaker. It was most peculiar, but with him standing there, leaning negligently against the mantelpiece, she had an oddly breathless feeling again, and she didn't like it. Because she was unsure of herself, and because subconsciously she wanted to test the strength of his determination to keep the peace – and some perverse feminine instinct was at work that she didn't understand either, she said: 'I suppose you're missing Laura, aren't you?'

He shrugged, almost amused it seemed, and took a swallow of his coffee before replying: 'As much as you're missing Mike, I imagine. Why do you ask?'

She shook her head, and a surge of that old bitter jealousy stung her with its dart. 'Aren't you worried that you can't see her? You don't know what she's doing – and Mike is slightly in l-love with her.'

She hoped to see his expression change; waited

almost breathlessly to see the answering jealousy in him. But she was disappointed. He raised an inquiring eyebrow. 'Well, well. The boy has more spirit than I gave him credit for. I wish him luck.' This with a wry grin.

Holly frowned. 'Don't you care?'

'Should I?' A thread of steel ran through his voice. But he wasn't angry – yet. She shook her head, puzzled, not strong enough to pursue it any further. Already she felt her hands tremble as she held the beaker. And Gareth said softly, almost gently: 'You really are a difficult little female, aren't you?'

'I don't understand what you—'

'Come *on*, Holly. Don't give me that wide-eyed stare of yours. Oh, it's very good, and no doubt it fools most of 'em – but I'm not one of the others. You were trying – very nicely, I admit – to needle me just then, weren't you? Let's see how far we can push old Gareth, hmm? After all, he's *said* he's not going to argue any more, so—' he crouched down suddenly in front of Holly. 'Right?'

'I don't know what you mean.' But the tongue licking her suddenly dry lips betrayed her, and he laughed.

'Yes, you do. And it won't work. I'm not going to get angry with you, or even slightly mad, because—' he eased himself on to the settee beside her – 'because you aren't yourself. You're about as strong as one of those ginger kittens I meant to have but didn't, and *I'd* be just about the most unfeeling brute in Scotland if I tangled with you now – and, despite all your ideas about me, I'm not that, I hope.' And as she looked down into her half-empty beaker of coffee, he tilted her chin very carefully round so that she faced him again.

'So you see, you can insult me all you like for the next day or so, and I shan't rise to the bait. Oh, I may go out into the kitchen and smash a few plates to relieve the frustration, but you—' and he tapped her chin lightly '—I shall leave strictly alone. Is that what it was all in aid of?'

She didn't answer for a moment, then: 'Y-yes, I suppose so. I'm – sorry.'

'Don't be. You're very young. You've a lot to learn in life, and if you never ask questions, you never find anything out. Just remember, though, there are different ways of finding out – and some are easier, and less painful, than others.' And with that cryptic remark, he stood up and left her alone while he went out to the kitchen. Holly sat very still, very quiet. The more she saw of Gareth, the less she felt she knew him. She also had the very disconcerting impression that he could read her as easily as an open book.

CHAPTER SEVEN

MONDAY passed, and Tuesday, and Holly regained her strength and ease of movement as she determinedly massaged her side with her aunt's liniment, and took a hot bath at night. Gareth, true to his word, was helpful and attentive, and quite impossible to annoy. Holly wondered how long he could keep it up. After all, it was not in his nature to be so pleasant and easy-going – at least not with *her*, she reasoned, and as he spent a lot of time on his writing, and had no way of unwinding to relax tension, somehow, somewhere, it was bound to build up.

And on Wednesday she became aware of the strain he was under, when, after sitting at the typewriter for two hours, he suddenly stood up and swept a pile of papers to the floor. There followed a few brief, unprintable epithets as he surveyed the littered carpet, while Holly sat frozen on the settee, not daring to speak.

After a few moments he moved away from the table, and wiped his hand wearily across his face. 'I apologize for the language,' he said abruptly.

'It's all right.' Holly stood and moved as if to the table. 'Let me—'

'No.' He shook his head. 'I'll sort them out. It's my problem.'

'But—' she began.

'I said *leave it*—' then as an afterthought, and with an effort: 'Thanks. If you want to help, get me a cup of coffee, will you?'

'Yes.' She hastened to the kitchen, and safely there, let out her breath in a deep sigh. She had known a slight difference in him that morning when he had come down – for once after her. His face had a drawn haggard look, as if he had slept badly. Holly was unaware of her own powers of attraction – oblivious of what was making him thus; that by the very nature of their enforced proximity, he was finding it increasingly difficult to concentrate in the face of his growing desire for her. The last few days had not helped matters. Since his decision not to argue during the time she was ill, he had had to repress his natural impulse to either kiss her or fight her. And now he had exploded. And Holly, as she made coffee, was aware that the situation, quite suddenly, had changed. She knew it wasn't for the better, but even she couldn't foresee the earth-shattering explosion that lay ahead, the foundations for which had already been laid, and towards which she and Gareth were inexorably moving.

She took in his coffee and handed him the beaker, watching him carefully as she did so. Some instinct warned her to be very cautious; a deep feminine intuition that was as old as time.

'Thanks.' And he turned away to go back to the table. He was wearing fine grey slacks and the off-white Aran sweater, and the indolent gipsy look had never been so strong. He looked tough, infinitely powerful – almost ruthless as he stood by the window looking out at the loaded grey skies. The snow had started an hour or so previously. Gentle flakes that looked as soft and innocent as swansdown – but had probably triggered off his mood. Perhaps he too felt as if they would be marooned for ever. Holly bit her lip, massaging her left arm, which was almost better. She watched him, her eyes taking in every inch of him with a kind of hungry intensity that both puzzled and dismayed her. His hair was blacker than night, his profile, etched against the window, dark and brooding, his chin jutting dangerously, a sure sign that his temper had returned. She looked away, and the room seemed darker by comparison. She switched on the lights, and told him: 'I'll get tea ready.'

'Right.' He didn't look round, and after a moment she went quietly out to the kitchen. Holly opened a large tin of mushroom soup and made toast, then set out plates. And she wished, not for the first time, that Aunt Margaret were there. It would be so much easier with the three of them. She bent to the grill and quickly removed the hot golden toast and began to butter it.

Then, just as she stirred the soup in the pan before removing it from the heat, all the lights went out, and the kitchen was plunged into premature gloom. 'Oh!' she gave an involuntary gasp of dismay and looked around, thinking for one absurd moment that Gareth had switched the lights off. Then she heard him moving across the living-room, and the next second he was a dark grey blur in the doorway.

'What the devil is it?' he said. 'The fuses?'

'I don't know. I hope so – because if it's not, it means the snow has cut the power lines, and that could be days – or weeks.'

'There's only one way to find out. Have you a torch? And where are the fuses?'

'Everything's in the pantry. I'll show you.' She turned and felt her way along the kitchen wall towards the pantry door, and heard the soft movements that told her he was behind her. She felt suddenly warm – and stifled. With a feeling of relief she found and opened the door and went into the cold dry atmosphere – now as black as pitch, for the pantry had no window. For a moment she stood still to get her bearings, and Gareth's hard body collided with hers, and his hands shot out to steady her. 'Sorry,' he said, and she felt his warm breath on her forehead as she half turned in panic.

'I don't – I don't know where a torch is for a moment,' she gasped. 'I was just trying to visualize.'

'I know. Just think now. Picture the torch. Is it in a drawer, a cupboard – or what?'

'Oh yes. Here, on the left. On the first shelf. There should be two.' She gingerly reached out her arm and patted it along the low shelf loaded with tins. The next moment a beam of light shot out, and she handed the torch to him. 'Here. The fuses are in the far corner.'

'Right. You stay there. If it is the snow, what other form of lighting have you?'

'There are four paraffin lamps in the other corner – and a full drum of paraffin. Aunt Margaret is always very careful about that. She's been cut off too many times to chance it. And there's a box of candles in the kitchen cupboard, and – oh yes, a paraffin stove in the barn for the dogs – only for emergencies like this, though.'

'We'll take one thing at a time. First I'll check the fuses, and then—' and he stopped as he made his way across by the neatly stacked tins and sacks and jars. 'Can you hold the torch?' he asked.

'Yes, of course.' Guided by the beam he directed at the floor for her, Holly joined him and crouched by his side as he knelt and lifted the cover from the fusebox.

A few minutes later they both knew the worst. He switched off at the mains, and she shot the beam into the far corner where the old familiar paraffin lamps were standing.

'They'll be full,' she told him. 'If you take two, we'll light them in the living-room.' In the sudden emergency, he had become cooler, more in control again, and she was thankful. But for how long, she wondered, would it last?

He put the cumbersome lamps on a coffee table by the fire, and touched the tall white shade with careful fingers. 'Beautiful,' he murmured. 'These would fetch a packet in a Bond Street store.'

Holly laughed. 'And they're years old. I remember being allowed to light them as a special treat when I was a little girl,' and the memory caught in her throat for a moment and she took a deep breath. Hastily, knowing she was talking about a time she didn't want to remember – at least, not with *him* there, she added: 'Will you light them?'

For a moment he looked at her, and the flickering gleam from the fire lit his face so that it blurred and moved, and the shadows grew dark behind him. Holly caught her breath at the expression she saw, just for a second. Then it was gone, and might never have been as he murmured: 'I'm afraid I haven't the faintest idea how.'

'Oh!' It startled her into silence. She heard him laugh softly.

'But I'm willing to learn. Here, let me hold the torch.' And as she passed it to him, their fingers touched, and it was like a sudden electric shock. She moved slightly away, then knelt and removed the cover as he held the beam steadily on the lamp, which caught and held the torchlight in its gleaming blue enamelled base.

Holly trimmed the wick, primed it, and as the match she had lit took hold with its yellow flame, she skilfully clipped the opaque glass shade into place. The cool yellow light bloomed and swelled in the room, and Gareth switched off the torch and put it down.

'Let me do the other one,' he said. 'And you can watch and tell me if I go wrong – in case I have to light them any time.'

'Yes, yes, of course.' She handed him the matches, but she was careful to let go of the box before their hands could touch, and she sat back and watched his careful, beginner's efforts with the second lamp. His fingers were long, the nails cut short and square and clean. She watched his hands fascinated, lit by the warmth of the other lamp, and in the silence as he worked, there came the faint hiss from it, as the wick greedily burnt the fuel to give them light.

'Okay? Did I do it right?' The light was doubled, the pool of yellow all around them, with flickering dancing shadows lurching crazily as he stood up. 'Where do they go?' he asked.

Holly pointed. 'One on the sideboard. The other on your table by the window. That way the whole room gets a share. If you want to read you can move one, though.' She put her hand to her mouth. 'Oh, I was doing soup! I'd better go or it won't be worth having.'

She picked up the second lamp and carried it out. You couldn't rush with one of them. You had to walk slowly and carefully, for they were quite heavy, and the sound of the paraffin splashing round inside the base could be disconcerting if you weren't used to it.

He followed her out. 'You should have let me,' he said. 'It's too heavy for you.'

She looked across at him. Strange, but this sort of light was oddly flattering to anyone. His skin was pale and shadowy, the features softened in the warmth – softened but not soft. There was nothing soft about him, she thought, as she reheated the soup on the gas. Concentrating on her task, she answered: 'But I'm better now. And I have lifted them before.'

'I know you're better. In fact, I was going to suggest moving back into my own house tomorrow—' and why did her heart lurch at that? '—but now—' he shrugged '—it might be safer here, together.'

'Y-yes, I suppose so.' She bit her lip. 'I might as well tell you then. Sometimes, when the weather's this bad – bad enough to cut the power off, I mean – the water goes off as well.'

He laughed. 'We'll worry about that when it happens. There's always snow to drink if the worst comes to the worst. Don't you ever have snowploughs trying to get through?'

'Oh, yes!' She poured the soup into the plates, and slid the toast on another. 'But even if it's cleared round Strathmhor, it's a few days before it gets to Kishard. There are so many places more important than us, you see.'

'But they'll be trying?' he persisted. She wondered why. Was he desperate to get away all of a sudden?

'Yes, they'll be trying. We just have to hope. I suggest we listen to the radio news tonight. If we only use it for that, it'll keep the battery going for ages. Excuse me. We'd better have this soup before it gets cold again.' And she walked quickly past him, stifling an irrational feeling of annoyance. What did she care if he couldn't wait to go? *She* hadn't asked him to come in the first place, *and* it would be a relief anyway, bad-tempered creature that he was . . .

They ate the toast and soup by the fire, and Holly had to shoo Kitty away, for she had come downstairs on hearing the clatter of crockery. The two cats spent most of their time sleeping at the foot of Gareth's bed, snuggled together for extra warmth. It was as if they were in a different house, sitting there as they were by a roasting fire, with the room lit solely by its flames, and the two lamps. Shadows were larger, moving quickly, dancing on the walls and window, and against the stairs. Everything was softer, the outlines of chairs and table less sharp. And Gareth. What was he thinking? she wondered, as he stood up to take their plates out. Was he affected too? Or was it, to him, merely something that had happened to delay him leaving for his own house? The truce brought about by the sudden shock of the electricity failure was fading, she knew. They had shared a crisis – and now it was over, or partly so – and she began to sense the difference in him, even in the way he moved as he returned.

The tension was building up again. It was there, in the set of his dark jaw, the angle of his head – and she wondered how she knew these things, as surely as if they were written for her to read. He was the enigmatic one, and yet – and Holly took a deep breath as realization washed over her. No longer, it seemed; no longer dark and mysterious. She, Holly, was vibrantly, vividly aware now of his slightest change of mood. And the knowledge was unnerving. But she knew why. In her innermost, secret heart, she knew why.

He spoke, shattering the brittle silence that had suddenly grown between them. 'I'll go and see to the dogs.'

And Holly remembered. 'The stove!' she looked up

quickly at him. 'The radiators will be cold. Oh, those poor animals!' In her agitation she stood up, and the paper serviette she had on her knee fluttered to the floor. 'We must light the heater for them.'

Gareth bent to pick up the serviette, and screwed it into a ball before throwing it on the fire. 'I'll do it. Do I fill it from the tin in the pantry?'

'Yes. But you won't manage alone. I'll—'

'I'll manage.' His voice was flat and decisive. 'If you'll prepare their food I'll take it out in the bucket. While you're mixing it, I'll go and get the heater lit.'

And he went into the kitchen, taking the torch with him. Holly followed, knowing it was useless to argue, but some perverse reaction to his words making her try anyway. 'I can come across with you. I'm better—'

He came out of the pantry with the huge tin, shadows dancing round him as the torch jogged up and down. 'I'll be back in a few minutes. It'll give me time to see if it's working properly, and heating the barn, before I feed them. Okay?' And he went without waiting for an answer.

Holly's mouth set in a rebellious line. She picked up a lamp and carried it out, set it down on the kitchen table with a bang, and began to prepare the animals' food. Smokey and Kazan, who had been deeply and soundly asleep in a warm corner by a radiator, came out sniffing, tails wagging hopefully.

She fed them first, put some of the meat aside for the cats, and began mixing the meat and meal in a large plastic bucket with a wooden spoon kept specially for the purpose. She stirred vigorously, dissipating some of the nervous energy which filled her. 'Who the hell does he think he is?' she muttered as she watched the dogs gulp their food, and she pounded the mixture in the bucket with her spoon. 'Giving all the orders – do this, do that!'

She set the bucket down on the floor, feeling like a rebellious schoolgirl. Suddenly on an impulse she couldn't – and didn't want – to define, she reached for a mac off the back door, slipped off her shoes, picked up the bucket and padded through the living-room in her stockinged feet to find a pair of wellingtons in the porch.

The cold air hit her with the force of a wall of ice. Gasping, realizing that this was the first time she had ventured out of doors since her fall, Holly pulled the mac more tightly round her, and took a deep breath. It would be nice to see the animals again. In any case, he had no business trying to tell her what to do, had he? Stumbling slightly as her wellingtoned foot skidded on a patch of ice, Holly made her way to the barn. The fresh snow that had fallen that afternoon glittered and sparkled like powdered diamonds in the clear moonlight, and nothing moved. And there was no sound in that cold sharp air, save the crunch of Holly's wellingtons as she walked, very carefully towards the barn. Then she heard the dogs as they welcomed Gareth, whining and snuffling round him. She saw the scene as she reached the doorway. He was bending over a large rectangular stove, taking the back off it. He looked up to see her, and his greeting was decidedly unwelcoming.

'I thought I told you to wait in the house,' he said.

'Yes, I know – but I thought I'd come anyway.' She said it quite pleasantly, because she didn't want to argue with him, but she wasn't taking orders from him either.

The dogs left Gareth and rushed over to her, smelling the food, and perhaps knowing that she had been missing and wanting to make up for the lost days. She bent down, trying not to laugh at the several warm tongues trying to lick her face. 'Oh, you're *all* lovely!' She patted as many as she could reach, and Herbert, the Afghan nearly knocked her flying in his enthusiasm. 'Whoa, all right! Come on, I'll feed you.' She stood up and reached round with her foot for the row of metal dishes that were now left in the barn beside the trough of water. She heard the soft hiss as the heater caught just as she began spooning the meat out for the hungry animals, and looked over at it, and the man bending over it, replacing the back firmly. Before he could turn to her, she bent quickly again, but her heart had begun to beat faster. Even though the light was so dim that nothing was clear – one thing was obvious, and that was Gareth's temper. I don't care! she thought rebelliously, giving the bucket a last scrape. Why should I care? But oddly, she did, and now she had made her brave, defiant gesture, she wanted nothing so much as to be back by a warm friendly fire in the living-room.

She heard the dogs gulping the food down, saw the dark shadowy shapes of them, and sensed Gareth's eyes on her.

'I'll – I'll go back now,' she said, and had to clear her throat. He didn't answer. After a moment she picked up the empty bucket and went to the door. The cold air hurt her throat and stung her cheeks with its sharp needles, and she hurried breathlessly back to the house.

She found herself waiting for Gareth to return – and some of her defiance evaporated as the minutes passed and there was still no sound, no sign of him. With an air of bravery she didn't really feel, she brewed a pot of tea, then sat drinking it by the fire which crackled and sparked as if nothing, anywhere, had ever been wrong.

Then, as the outer door opened, Holly stiffened. She cradled the cup of tea in her hands, and waited for the explosion. For she knew in her bones, with that sure new instinct, that he was angry – and that he would not let it pass.

He came in and shut the door behind him. Then he crossed to the fire, and looking down at Holly, said: 'I wasn't telling you to stay in here just to be bossy. I was doing it because you could easily have slipped and fallen again – and you'd probably have broken something.'

It wasn't what she had expected. And because he seemed almost calm – almost, she was stung to retort: 'Well, I didn't. I walked carefully across, and I had wellingtons on this time – and anyway, I needed some fresh air.'

He gave a small crooked smile. 'Fresh? It's that all right. You could stand at an open window for five minutes if fresh air's all you want.'

Holly stood up restlessly and put her cup on the mantelpiece. Tension she could not define was building in her and she felt stifled. For some reason of his own, he was controlling his temper almost visibly, and the temptation within her was to goad him. Why, she could not imagine, but something drove her on.

'*You* wouldn't understand,' she answered breathlessly. 'I'm sick of being cooped up here all the time, with – with just you.'

'Really?' A sharper edge came into his voice, and her heart pounded. 'And how do you think I feel? It's not exactly a picnic for me.'

'I didn't ask you to come,' she retorted. 'I would have managed.'

'Like hell you would!' They stood facing each other like two boxers in a ring, still wary, mentally circling ready for the skirmish. This had been destined, ever since he had set foot in the house to help her, and if it hadn't been about this it would have been about something else, for the strains of living together in the close confines of a house, unchaperoned, were taking their inevitable toll. And so Holly faced him, ready for battle – but she couldn't possibly have dreamed of what was to come, of the truths that were also inevitable, in their own way.

'I've coped before.' Her eyes were large and dark in the soft light, and they met his own infinitely darker ones unblinkingly. 'I stayed here often when I was a child. I'd have managed all right – *you* don't even know how to light a paraffin lamp.' And she tried a laugh, but it didn't quite come off. And he knew. Very softly, he said:

'I see you'll be getting down to personal insults next – but then that's understandable. After all, you are only a child. Eighteen, is it?'

'I'm a woman – as I'm sure you're well aware,' she shot back. 'You – you weren't kissing a *child* that night in the Land-Rover, you know. But of course, you had that little incident well planned, didn't you?' She mimicked him accurately: ' "I'm afraid I don't carry a spare can of petrol," – it's a wonder Mike didn't fall over it when he got in!'

'Carry on, you're doing fine. Get all the venom off your chest – I can take it,' he remarked almost casually. 'You must be getting better. Those little kitten claws of yours are sharpening up nicely. I'll bet you never let Mike see them, though, did you? After all, the Colonel is pretty wealthy – you could do a lot worse.'

'How dare you!' Holly nearly choked.

'Oh, come *on* now! It's my turn, remember? I'm a bit out of practice with insults, but it's coming back to me – and you look as if you enjoy a good slanging match. You should just see your face, Holly.' He reached out and ran his hand roughly down her cheek, and she knocked it away quickly. He laughed. 'That's better. Got a bit of fire back too. I'm sorry for Mike, he doesn't know what he's in for.'

'Nor does Laura – if *you* take after your *father*!' she spat out. She saw his face change, heard the quick in-drawn hiss of breath, and she knew she had gone just too far. A strange exultation filled her. At last she had got through that steely control. At last – and then she heard the most puzzling words she had ever heard in her life.

'And *you* take after your *mother* – oh yes, very much so.'

His face was hard and like a stranger's, and the words were unbelievably bitter and intense.

'*What did you say?*' she mouthed, very slowly and carefully, as if something terrible was about to happen – and she knew that it was.

'You heard me.' Each word was clipped and precise. 'You heard me very well. I said you take after your mother. Don't tell me she didn't tell you?'

'Tell me what?' Holly thought she was going to fall over, but something made her stand up straighter than before. 'You'd better tell me what you mean.'

'With pleasure. But you might need to sit down. You're going to have a few shocks.' He stood very straight and tall, and Holly shook her head.

'I don't need to sit down for anything *you* have to tell me.'

The light was soft and mellow – but it had a dangerous quality, as if the air was filled with the something terrible about to come.

And as he said his next words, Holly knew why. 'You think of my father as a bitter, cruel man,' he said, his voice intense and hard. 'And perhaps he was, and is – and we all know your side of the story, so I'll balance it now with mine. He had a reason for what he did – I'm not saying he was right, but it's time you knew anyway. Your mother was about to marry my father, when he introduced her to his good friend James Templeton. Two weeks later they ran away and married. If that hadn't happened, she would have been my stepmother.'

Holly's face was ashen. 'I don't believe you,' she whispered. 'You're a liar.'

Shadows played on his face, but his eyes darkened dangerously even so. 'Do you think I would lie about a thing like that?'

'Y-you did about your name.'

'No. I merely left off "Greene" when I moved here. I had my reasons.'

'I still don't believe you. You're making it up out of – of spite,' she managed. But she had to lean on the mantelpiece for support now. 'You're vicious and cruel – like *him*.' She forced the words out, and it was a terrible effort, but she had to go on – she had to *know*.

He was breathing hard, as if he had been running, as if it was a terrible effort for him too – but it was also as if, having started, he couldn't, or wouldn't stop until all was said. 'She was my father's secretary. He had a small office then – hardly any money. I'm going back twenty-one years. She – your mother – worked for my father, and he made the big mistake of letting her meet your father—' a bitter smile fleetingly touched his mouth '—and your father was already wealthy. She didn't tell you *that*, did she—'

His words were cut off abruptly as Holly, with a desperate harsh anger, launched herself at him, to silence the words she could no longer bear – that she could no longer take.

'You – I *hate* you, you despicable, loathsome—' Sobbing, she reached up for his face, her nails raking down his cheek, because at that moment she really did hate him. Then she felt herself being caught and held and thrust backwards so that she was pressed against the wall beside the fireplace, and Gareth was gripping her with a strength she had not imagined any man could possess. 'You're hurting me – let me—' she struggled vainly, saw the fury in his eyes, and gasped.

'I'd like to hurt you – by God I'd like to!' he breathed. His face was white in contrast with the three red stripes down his left cheek, and Holly, mingled with all the other sensations, felt fear of his infinite power.

'You don't like to hear the truth, do you?' he grated. 'You can't stand *that*! It might destroy the precious dream world you live in. Well, it's time you grew up and learned a few facts of life. And one is that things aren't always one-sided – there are two, often more, sides to everything. I don't get on with my father. We've quarrelled so many times about his business – about everything he does in life – that eventually I left home to go my own way. Twenty years ago he had a thousand pounds in the bank, and a young son to feed – but he believed in hard work. He was shattered when your mother left, just like that—' he released one hand to click his fingers contemptuously '—so he determined to show them both that he was better than *everybody*. And he did. All right, so he was vengeful. He did what no decent man would do. He moved in on your father and ruthlessly sent him to the wall. I don't agree with him for that, but *he* felt as if he had a reason – and I'll bet your mother told you everything else, but not that deep-down truth.' He released her abruptly as if wearying of words, and she nearly fell to the floor. She felt drained of life, completely shattered, and barely able to move.

Gareth turned away. But he had not finished. He looked back and then touched his raw cheek carefully. 'You're spoilt and childish,' he said. 'And don't hit me again like that – ever – or you'll regret it.'

Holly found a trace of spirit to enable her to answer him. 'I don't w-want to touch you again,' she answered. 'You're loathsome.' She was breathing rapidly, trying to absorb the shock, to take in the words which were so unbelievable that they would not sink in for a long time. She felt cold too, as if the fire had died down, and she looked quickly at it, but it was high and bright and crackling merrily. She shivered, and with a great effort, pulled herself away from the wall. Her eyes were aching, but she was determined not to cry. She would *not* cry – not in front of him – ever again. On legs that wobbled, she went out to the kitchen to get a glass of water to ease her parched throat which ached with the terrible words she had heard. She didn't look back as she went out, and she didn't see Gareth smash his clenched fist against the hard mantelpiece in a kind of quiet despair. If she had, she would not have understood why; that would have been something beyond even her comprehension.

She took the water upstairs with her, filled her hot-water bottle in the bathroom, and went to bed, there to sleep the long, almost dreamless sleep of utter exhaustion. Gareth had still been standing by the fireplace when she had walked through, and there could have been a mile-high wall between them. Her heart was dead within her, all feelings for him extinguished in a numb sort of shock that she thought would never go away.

The next morning, when she went down, the room was cold, the fire long dead. Smokey and Kazan were curled up on the settee fast asleep, and both jumped guiltily when she came in, and slid off. Holly went to the back door and opened it, expecting the usual blast of icy air to hit her. Instead she saw a faint watery sun gleaming on the snow, and the air, though cold, had less of a freezing quality. Perhaps there would be a thaw. Maybe, soon, a snowplough would get through and release her from what had become an intolerable situation. Perhaps . . . She shivered and went to clear the fireplace ready to light the fire. Gareth had been doing that task since his arrival, but she was determined never to speak, or ask anything of him ever again. She could not accept his words, the dreadful things he had said the previous night. And she knew now that she could no longer live at Rhu-na-Bidh. When the snow had gone; when Aunt Margaret returned, Holly would leave. And as long as *he* was there, she would not come back. Holly knew it would break her heart, for she loved her aunt dearly, but now she knew how cruel, how intolerable Gareth could be, there would be no peace for her at the cottage as long as he remained. Somehow the resolution helped her. It was as if she had made a long-delayed decision, and thus set her mind at rest.

She heard his footsteps on the stairs as she put a match to the firelighters, and she stiffened. There was only one more thing to do – to *prove* – with Gareth, and when that was done, she was finished with him.

She knew he was in the room, but she didn't turn round. Instead she watched the crackling wood beginning to catch and spark, the spurts of yellow flame shooting up. And when she was sure that it would burn properly, she stood up. Without looking round, she went to the small bookcase in the corner by the window, and from it she took an old family Bible. Then she looked at him. His face shocked her. He looked as if he had not slept at all. Nor had he shaved, and the black stubble, and the three vivid scratches on his cheek, served to accentuate the almost piratical look about him. Before she could weaken, Holly thrust the Bible at him. 'Take it,' she said, 'and swear on it – if you can – that you spoke the truth last night.' Her voice was calm and level. She had had a lot of time to think about this, and she was so drained of all emotion that it became easier with every moment that passed.

'No,' he said. 'No, I won't.'

'Because you lied?' Her breath caught in her throat.

'No. I spoke the truth. It's not that. It's that I – I shouldn't have told you in the way I did. I had no right to do it. I was—' he paused '—I told you in a brutal way I regret very much.'

'I don't care. I don't *want* you to be sorry – I just

want to know *if it was the truth.*'

'Yes – yes, it was.' He hesitated, she saw his clenched jaw, then, as if coming to a decision, he added: 'Your aunt will tell you. She knows – she has known for twenty years how your mother and father met.' He stopped at Holly's wordless cry of pain, and she put the Bible on the table, blindly, unseeing.

'That's why – she told me I must not leave, that day you discovered who I – really was.' He stood there, and on his face was the look of a man in torment. For the very first time since she had met him, Holly saw deep pain in his features. But it was nothing compared to her own, and she felt almost a savage streak of pleasure that something had managed to hurt him at last.

She took a deep breath. 'I don't ever want to speak to you again,' she said. 'And when my aunt returns home I shall go away, for I shall not live here, with you as a neighbour, any more.' And she turned and walked steadily and with great dignity to the kitchen.

His voice halted her as she reached the door, but she never looked back. 'You needn't go. If anyone should leave, it's me. I accept that. Don't worry, once the road is passable you won't see me again.'

Holly waited, to see if there was any more, and then, when there wasn't, she went out to make toast for herself. She didn't feel hungry or thirsty. She didn't feel anything, except a great yawning misery within her that refused to go away.

CHAPTER EIGHT

ONCE, during the day, when Holly was at the back door to let the cats out, she heard the distant sound of an engine, and stood still to listen. It could have been miles away, for any noise carried long distances in that clear cold air. She closed her eyes for a moment, wondering if it was a snowplough at last. Oh, if only it were! With a sigh she turned away and began to wash the dishes.

She and Gareth had not exchanged a word since morning. The two dogs were unhappy about it, sensing the painful atmosphere, and were now huddled miserably together in a corner on a warm blanket, keeping well out of the way. There was nothing Holly could do about it, she knew, but it didn't help her either. Gareth was at his table typing, occasionally stopping to write something, or refer to one of the pile of diaries and notebooks that lay in front of him, and Holly busied herself in work, for she wanted not to have to think, now above all. He had said he would leave – very well, let him, she thought, unable however hard she tried, to make her mind a blank. Then she would never *ever* see him again as long as she lived, and perhaps she would marry Mike – and then she remembered Laura. What of her? What if she and Gareth married each other? That would make them cousins-in-law! No, he wouldn't – or if he did, they would live in a city. Mike had assured her that Laura would not settle in the wilds for long. Perhaps even now she was desperate to get away – but not without seeing her lover, of course.

Holly, busy making scones as a change from bread, paused in her mixing for a moment. She wondered what would happen. It was quite possible that Gareth would be swept off his feet on seeing her again, especially *now* – after all that had happened, after all the bitterness, the unhappiness of the present situation. With a sigh she bent vigorously to mixing again. It did not, it *must not* matter, she must stop thinking about him . . .

And then she heard the most unbelievable of noises – a knock at the front door. Wiping floury hands on her apron, she ran quickly through, saw Gareth about to get up, and without a word to him, crossed the room and flung the door open.

Mike stood there, swaddled like an Eskimo, and covered in powdered snow.

'Mike – oh, Mike!' Delighted, never more thankful to see anyone, Holly pulled him into the room and looked at him with shining eyes. 'How on earth did you do it?' she gasped.

He pulled a face. 'It's taken me nearly an hour – over the hill, through the wood. I found an old pair of skis in the garage and thought I'd have a go.' He glanced across and saw Gareth for the first time, and if he was surprised, he knew how to hide it. 'Hi! Didn't see you. Doesn't it go dark quickly?' He reached in his pocket. 'I've a letter for you from Laura,' and he pulled it out.

Gareth took it from him. 'Thanks, Mike. Excuse me, will you? I'll go and see to the dogs in the barn.'

And he went out quietly, unsmiling now after that brief answering one to Mike's.

Mike waited until the door had closed behind Gareth, then gave a low whistle. 'Wow! What's up with *him*? He looks as if he's been out on the tiles or something.'

Holly shook her head. 'I can't tell you, Mike. But we're not speaking. I – I don't want to talk about it. Sorry.' She swallowed hard. 'Let me make you a hot drink. What will it be? Coffee, tea, cocoa? We've got them all. Made with powdered milk, of course.'

'Of course! Any will do,' he grinned. 'We're down to condensed milk now – in everything. Ugh! It'll be a pleasure to taste the other.' He followed her into the kitchen, and as she switched on the gas she said: 'I'll just pop these scones in the oven while you're waiting, then you can take a few back with you. How are you managing?'

He laughed. 'Not too bad. Due entirely to our valued housekeeper, I might add. She's a Scot, she'd stocked up with most of the things we need, and Dad is so grateful – honestly, the old boy's a changed man. He doesn't bark at her any more, he *requests* her, gently. Scared she'll leave, I think.'

Holly smiled, deftly cutting out the shapes as she listened. It was like a breath of fresh air, him coming as he had, and her spirits lightened. He had taken the hint about Gareth apparently, though he wouldn't be human if he didn't wonder . . .

They talked, and drank their coffee by the fire, and Gareth hadn't returned even an hour later, when Mike reluctantly looked at his watch, and said: 'Look, I'll have to go soon, Holly, though I don't want to, but I need some light to see my way.'

'Of course. Oh, Mike, it's been wonderful to have you.' She stood and went across to the lamps and lit them both as he began to stir, looking round for his coat. 'Will you take a tin of dried milk with you? A present?'

'No, thanks, Holly. I might try the village tomorrow – might even rig up a sled – and anyway, I heard something like a loud tractor today, and our housekeeper, who should know, assured us it was a snowplough.'

'Oh, I hope so,' Holly murmured. 'I hope so.' She went out to the kitchen to put a few scones in a bag, and when she returned, Mike was standing with his coat on, fastening it up. She went forward to help him, and he put his arms round her and kissed her.

'Oh, Mike,' she put her head against the warm furry coat, and gave a sigh of utter despair. 'Oh, Mike!'

He gripped her arms. 'Holly! What is it? It's Gareth, isn't it?'

She looked at him, her eyes bright with the tears that refused to fall. 'Yes, it is. He's so – so—' she gasped, and turned as the door opened, frightened, seeing Gareth walk in, tall, tough, unsmiling. And the light from the table fell on his face, illumining the dark deep scratches, and she felt Mike stiffen, heard his indrawn breath as he said: 'I didn't notice those before.' The two men's glances locked and Holly could almost feel the tension mounting in the room as Mike said to him: 'What the hell have you been doing to Holly?'

Gareth shrugged. 'Why don't you ask her?' His eyes were black and frightening, and Holly clutched Mike's arm in fear.

'Leave it, Mike, please.'

'Like hell I will!' He shook himself free. 'Holly jumped like a frightened mouse the second you came in, and you're covered in scratches on your face – what am I supposed to be thinking? You didn't get *those* for nothing.'

'No? Then what do *you* suppose I got them with?' Gareth walked slowly nearer, broad-shouldered, infinitely menacing, his voice soft – a dangerous sign, Holly knew, but Mike did not. 'Tell me. I could do with a good laugh.'

'You don't need it spelling out, do you? First it's Laura, now Holly – you're a real swift mover, aren't you?' Mike wiped the back of his hand across his mouth. 'I've a good mind to punch you on the nose—'

'No, Mike!' Then Holly heard Gareth laugh, almost as if amused, and her blood chilled.

'I don't fight,' he said coolly. 'I don't believe in violence. I'm going up to my room. I suggest you calm down.'

His words had the oddest effect on Holly. She felt almost sick, and seeing him walk across the room to the stairs, she said in a loud clear voice: 'I shouldn't bother with him, Mike – he's a coward.'

Gareth stopped with his foot on the bottom step. He half turned and looked directly at Holly. 'You can think what you like,' he said. And then he went. For a few moments there was utter silence in the room, as they heard his footsteps upstairs, heard his bedroom door shut firmly.

Mike took a deep breath. 'My God,' he whispered. 'Don't tell me he's sleeping here!'

'Yes. But it's not what it seems, Mike. Those scratches – he told me something about my mother, something I couldn't take. And he only moved in because I slipped in the snow and hurt myself. He – he's not touched me, I swear it.' Her body trembled helplessly, and Mike drew her into the shelter of his arms.

'Oh, you poor kid,' he breathed. 'I'm sorry, Holly.'

He looked up hopelessly at the ceiling. 'I knew there was something badly wrong when I came here. I'm sorry, I thought he'd tried to take advantage—'

A half sob rose in Holly's throat. 'Oh, no, not that. I h-hate him,' she whispered, and clenched her fists together helplessly. 'I hate him!'

Mike looked at her, and for a moment there shone knowledge beyond his years in his eyes. 'Do you, Holly? Do you *really*?'

'I don't understand,' she breathed.

'I think perhaps you do.'

'No – *no*!' But even as she said the words of denial, her pulse quickened, and she looked at him with something like despair. 'What am I going to do, Mike?' she begged. 'Am I going mad?'

He squeezed her gently. 'No, I don't think so. You look very sane – and very lovely, to me.' And he smiled. 'I'm going now, love. I'll come again as soon as I can, don't worry.'

'You are a good friend.' She touched his arm softly.

'I know, I know,' he gave a twisted grin. 'And you know something? I'm going to go home and make a big effort in a certain direction. When I say what I've got to say, I think somehow I might get a slightly warmer reception than previously.' And with those rather puzzling words, he went to the door. And he refused to tell Holly, despite her pleas, exactly what he meant.

She knew that she loved Gareth, in spite of everything – she had known all along. But was it so obvious that Mike had seen it? Restlessly Holly turned in bed that night, alternately hot, then shivering as if with a fever. She put her hand to her burning forehead. That it should be him, of all men, that she should fall in love with. Unable to sleep, she sat up and pulled her dressing-gown over her shoulders.

There was no sound from her aunt's bedroom. Gareth had gone back to his own house next door. He had waited until Mike had left, then come down with some clothes in a bundle. Just before opening the front door, he had said: 'I'm moving out. I'll get the rest of my things in the morning. I'll feed the dogs and see to them tonight. Please leave the food in the porch about nine. I'll collect it.' And he had gone. His face when he spoke had been expressionless; pale and tired and still unshaven, as if he didn't give a damn – and maybe he didn't any more.

Holly had not answered, just watched him leave, imagining him going into that freezing house next door, and her throat ached with some emotion she could not express. Something had made her go to the porch later. The smoke curled up in a thin spiral, and a faint light shone out of the window. So he had warmth, and he had found a lamp. Holly had turned away, knowing the ache in her heart was one she would carry for a long time . . .

Now, restlessly she crept downstairs and made a pot of tea, taking a brimming beaker back up with her. The house was eerily silent, and she knew loneliness again, this time differently from before.

She drank the tea, then lay down, hoping that she would sleep, and perhaps forget, if only for a few hours.

She dreamed a vivid dream about the dogs being attacked by a wolf from the mountains, and they all started barking furiously as it crept stealthily along and into the barn. Barking in a riotous cacophony of sound that grew louder and louder . . .

Holly sat up, knocking the beaker flying as she realized that the barking was real. It wasn't a dream now, something was wrong. She groped for her slippers in the dark, fumbled for the torch, and slipping her dressing-gown on, ran quickly downstairs. She must get to the barn. Kicking off her slippers, she put her bare feet into a pair of freezing cold wellingtons standing in the porch, and started running across the yard. The acrid smell of burning drifted across to her as she stumbled her way.

As she reached the barn, she stopped dead at the sight which met her eyes.

A smoke-blackened figure was coming out carrying two yelping, terrified dogs. Quickly she rushed forward, the initial shock over.

'I'll take them!' she shouted. Gareth handed them to her, the two smallest of the lot, and she grabbed desperately.

'In the run – put them in the run!' he called, vanishing into the smoke-filled doorway. She obeyed, dropped the frightened animals in the wire-enclosed run, and rushed back to the door. This time he dragged Herbert out. The Afghan was yelping miserably, and a singed patch on his back leg told its own story. 'All right,' she promised him as she pushed him into the run and shut the gate. 'I'll attend to it later.'

Ten minutes later all the dogs were safely out and Holly ran inside the barn.

'Where the hell are you going?' Gareth dragged her roughly out.

'There's a fire extinguisher on the wall just inside—' she began.

'Right or left?'

'Left. But—' But he had gone. The smoke was acrid, choking and dense, and she followed him in, switching on her torch to help. There was a small fire going in the centre of the floor, where the stove lay on its side, but by a miracle there was no straw near it, nothing for the flames to catch on to and spread, although sparks were flying up to the roof – and then a jet of white foam shot out towards the brightly burning stove, and Gareth went nearer, coughing, taking huge gasping breaths as he ordered Holly to get out. She stood her ground. Nothing in the world would make her leave him now – he would have to knock her down first, and drag her out . . . She coughed, the acid-smelling fumes from the foam mixing with the smoke, and it was hard to say which was worse—

'I think it's all out. Shine that torch – no, over there, that's it.' He stamped vigorously a few times on the stone floor, and put the extinguisher down. 'Let's get out of here—' His next words were lost in a fit of coughing as he came over and propelled Holly out before him. They stood in the doorway gulping sweet fresh air thankfully.

'I think it's all out. I'll come back in a few minutes with a bucket of water and check.' But he staggered slightly as he said it, and put his arm on the door arch for support.

'There's a snow shovel outside,' said Holly. She was calmer now, more in control of herself. 'I'll heave some snow in and spread it round. It'll help prevent anything starting.'

'Good idea. Where is—'

'I'll get it. Please go into the house. You're not—' then she saw his arm in the light from the torch, and gasped: 'You're hurt!'

He looked at his arm disinterestedly, as if it belonged to someone else. 'Fancy that! Your concern is deeply touching. *Where's the shovel?*'

She swallowed hard, reached round outside the door, and picked it up. The next quarter of an hour was spent in spreading and flattening snow on the floor of the now cold, smelly, and slippery barn.

When they had finished he flung the shovel down. 'That's it. Now, the animals. They can come in my house for the rest of the night.'

'No. My aunt's. I want to check if any are hurt first. I know the Afghan is, on his leg. Please.'

He shrugged. 'As you wish.'

They began to carry or push the thoroughly cowed, miserable dogs into the house, where Kazan and Smokey added to the general upheaval by greeting the newcomers with loud barking. Eventually the last one was in and Holly shut the front door with a sigh of relief. Gareth sat on the settee, exhausted, with only the dim glimmer from a nearly dead fire, and the light from the torch, giving any illumination to the room, now overrun with excited animals sniffing round at their new surroundings. Holly quickly lit the lamps, then stood before him.

'Please let me look at your arm,' she said. 'You've been bitten, haven't you?'

'It looks like it,' he surveyed the swollen blackened skin above his wrist dispassionately. 'The poor devils were scared stiff.'

Holly knelt before him, uncaring that she was pleading now, wanting – *needing* only to help him. 'Now,' she said, 'come in the kitchen. A dog bite can be dangerous. I must clean it now. *Please.*'

For a second she caught a glimpse of the old sardonic

amusement, then: 'I never thought I'd see you begging on your knees to me,' he remarked bitterly. 'Don't tell me you care, after all?'

Holly was nearly crying. 'Please,' she begged. 'What can I say? Please come now, then I can look at the dogs—'

'Ah, I see.' He stood up. 'You only want to get rid of me so that you can look after the dogs. Well, that's fair enough, but why didn't you say so before?'

She carried the lamp into the kitchen and set it down by the sink. Then she ran warm water into the bowl, and reached for the Dettol. Gareth still wore his pyjama top, tucked loosely into blue jeans. The sleeve was nearly torn off. He sat on the stool by the sink, and Holly began bathing his arm with antiseptic, soaking a clean tea-towel because there was nothing else handy, and she didn't like the blue-black bruises around the bite . . .

He sat very still, and then he looked quickly up at Holly, and surprised the expression on her face before she could wipe it away.

He said softly: 'You really are worried, aren't you?'

She looked at him, and something in his glance turned her bones to jelly. 'Yes,' she whispered, 'I am.'

'Then,' he said slowly, 'I'd better tell you something. You can get tetanus from a dog bite, can't you?' Holly nodded.

'*I* won't – if that's what's concerning you. I was bitten about four years ago, and had a tetanus shot then. I kept them up afterwards, to give me lifetime immunity. I've even got a little orange card in my wallet to prove it.'

'I – I—' Holly felt the tears of relief spring to her eyes, tears she had sworn she would never shed in front of him. 'Oh.' She closed her eyes, and one tear escaped and trickled down to her chin, where it hovered for a moment before dropping into the bowl.

'Why are you crying?' he said in a strange voice, and he wanted an answer.

She shook her head, blinking hard, desperately. 'I – I'm tired, that's all,' and there was something she had to tell him now, before it was too late. 'I called you a coward yesterday,' she said with an effort, and although she had paused in her bathing, she still held his arm – and was quite unaware of the fact. 'I'm sorry. You're not. After what you just did – but I didn't even think you were before. I just wanted to hurt you, if I c-could.'

He looked at her. 'Being called a coward didn't hurt me. There was a reason why I wouldn't fight him. Do you want to know what it was?'

'No,' she shook her head. 'No, there's no need—'

'There is a need.' His voice was harsh, and his eyes held hers now, and Holly couldn't have looked away for anything. 'Because – if I had touched him, I would have half killed him – because what he said, or thought, was true in a way.' He stopped.

'But he thought—' whispered Holly.

'He thought I'd been trying to make love to you. He didn't know how damn near right he was—' Holly heard his breathing become harder, and his voice was husky as he went on: 'Because if I'd stayed here another night – I—' he groaned, and turned his head away. 'Oh, God, what's the use? I've already made a fool of myself. I might as well finish it. I know you hate me – I know what your feelings are. Well, here's something you can have a really good laugh about. Mike was jealous. He had a right to be, because I want you more than anything – more than words can tell.' He gave a wry, bitter laugh. 'Right? Start laughing. I can take it – I can take anything after today.' And she knew he wasn't referring to the fire.

'I thought I hated you,' she said slowly. 'I wanted to, because of everything – but I can't,' she felt her legs buckling with fatigue, but she knew she had to finish, to rid herself of the intolerable ache within her heart. 'And Mike guessed. He told me – oh, not in so many words, but his meaning was clear – that he knew I l-loved you.' And the tears came then, blessed tears that fell freely because at last she had spoken what was in her heart, without fear.

Wordlessly he stood, took her in his arms. And kissed her.

Minutes later, her voice muffled as she spoke into his chest, she said: 'The dogs – shouldn't we see to the dogs?'

'In a minute.' He cradled her roughly in his arms. 'Oh, Holly, I love you. I always have.' And then he held her slightly away as he asked in surprised tones: 'Do you think your Aunt Margaret knew?'

'Oh!' she began to laugh. 'Oh, yes, I'm sure she did. Little things she said – oh yes!' Holly nodded happily, her whole being content.

Later, after she had bandaged Gareth's arm, seen that the dogs were all right, and dressed the fortunately slight burn on Herbert's leg – and decided that he had caused the fire – Holly sat with Gareth on the settee, the fire glowing brightly, surrounded by ten dogs of assorted colours and sizes, some sleeping, some awake. And the time came for talking.

'Two questions I must ask,' Holly said, and looked at him, watching the firelight playing on his beloved features – beloved now – an enemy no more.

'Fire away, Holly,' and he smiled, and held her tightly.

'Well, first – how did it happen that you came here, of all places? Was it coincidence?'

'Not exactly. We used to come here for holidays – near Kishard, I mean, when my mother was alive. She was killed in a car crash when I was eight. I've always remembered this place with affection – you never know, your father and mine may have found they had this place in common when they eventually met, in the Army. Anyway, when I decided I'd had enough of the rat race, I made for here. I swapped my Jaguar in Inverness, bought a Land-Rover, and drove on here. In Kishard I asked if anyone had property to rent or sell, and the woman at the post office told me of your aunt. I'll admit it, I came mainly out of curiosity at first – the name Templeton is unusual – but I was completely bowled over by your aunt the minute I met her, and nothing else seemed to matter. Gradually, as the weeks passed, I discovered her connection with your father – and I decided to say nothing. What good would it have done? Then I met you – and the rest you know.'

'Yes,' she smiled softly. 'And – Laura?'

'Ah, yes.' He took a deep breath. 'It was not – as it seemed,' and as she stirred involuntarily, he squeezed her tighter, continuing: 'What I mean is – and I'll be blunt – I was never in love with her, not even slightly, and I never made love to her. Is that what you wanted to know?'

'Yes, but—' she began.

'But nothing! Sure, I was out with her to all hours,

but she was just someone – good amusing company – and I was beginning to need company, believe me – to go out with, spend my money on. And that's *all*, little carrot top.'

'Oh! There's one more – no, never mind,' she added hastily, seeing the glint in his eye and shivering deliciously.

'Go on, you minx. Don't stop *now*!'

'Well, when I first came – there was a letter one day, from France, and I – but I mustn't—'

He began to laugh. 'Oh, Holly! I do believe you're jealous! I'll show you that letter, when I find it. The writer – yes, it is a woman – was a very good – er – friend of my grandfather, the one I'm writing the biography of. She's eighty-one!' He stretched. 'Oh, I'll tell you all about him some time. He was a fascinating old man, explorer, engineer, inventor – everything. We got on well, the two of us – and he left me all his money,' he looked apologetically at Holly. 'So I need never work again,' and as she stirred guiltily, he added softly: 'Unless you call running an animal sanctuary work!' He stood up abruptly. 'I think we both deserve a drink. What say you?'

Holly rose. 'There's some sherry in the kitchen, I think,' she said, 'I'll go and see.'

A few minutes later they each held a glass half filled with Aunt Margaret's best sherry, a rather sweet Australian wine that was very pleasant, and Gareth raised his glass.

'A toast to Aunt Margaret,' he said. 'For she knew – bless her – and she did something about it, in her way, by moving out and leaving us to slog it out together.'

'Hear, hear,' Holly murmured sleepily, and they drank.

'And to Herbert, for starting the fire, because if he hadn't, we'd never have known either.'

'Herbert,' Holly agreed solemnly. Gareth's arm round her was warm and strong, and just right. It was nearly six o'clock in the morning, night was fading slightly, and in the distance they heard the faint engine noise again. Gareth raised his glass. 'And to the snow-plough that's coming slowly but surely to the rescue – because it will save me fighting a way through the snow to see the vicar, because I refuse to stay in the same house with Holly Templeton much longer without a marriage licence.' Then he stopped, and put his glass down, and gently took Holly's from her.

'I mean it, my sweet little kitten,' he told her quietly. 'All joking apart, I love you so very, very much. We have a lot of things to learn, both of us, but we will, and it will be all right, and we'll be married, for I can't live without you.' His dark, vital gipsy face was so near, and Holly reached up to touch his cheek, and she said, very softly:

'I love you too, Gareth. Where will we live after – when we're married?'

He grinned. 'Where else? Next door – and Holly, you know, I've got quite a soft spot for Herbert. If he's not claimed – and I hope now he won't be – can we—'

'Keep him? Oh, Gareth, what a wonderful idea!'

They were still laughing when the snowplough came along the main road at the foot of the track.